SELECTED WRITINGS

MIRJAM TUOMINEN

SELECTED WRITINGS

TRANSLATED BY
David McDuff

INTRODUCTION BY
Tuva Korsström

BLOODAXE BOOKS

ISBN: 1 85224 218 3

First published 1994 by
Bloodaxe Books Ltd,
P.O. Box 1SN,
Newcastle upon Tyne NE99 1SN.

Bloodaxe Books Ltd acknowledges
the financial assistance of Northern Arts.

ACKNOWLEDGEMENTS
Acknowledgements are due to the Arts Council of England
for providing a translation grant for this book, and to *Books
from Finland* where some of these translations were first published.
The Swedish texts used for this translation were taken from
Mirjam Tuominen i urval I-III (Söderström & C:o, Helsingfors,
1989, 1990, 1991), with additional material from *Tema med
variationer* (1952), *Under jorden sjönk* (1954) and *Dikter III* (1956),
all originally published by Söderströms.

Cover printing by J. Thomson Colour Printers Ltd, Glasgow.

Printed in Great Britain by
Cromwell Press Ltd, Broughton Gifford, Melksham, Wiltshire.

Contents

INTRODUCTION

I write it shows in the eyes of the dog
it creeps in the paw of the cat
it shimmers in the solitary fly's pair of wings
it leaps in foaling withers
it flies in the flight of birds
it flies
it sinks
into the earth down under roots
it smiles in the infant's eyes
it grows in the eyes of children
it wonders in young eyes
it yearns in human eyes.

The 25-year-old Mirjam Irene Tuominen made her début in 1938 with a collection of short stories, *Tidig tvekan* (Early Hesitation). Hagar Olsson, Edith Södergran's friend and the leading Finland-Swedish critic, gave the book an enthusiastic review:

> With her collection of short stories Mirjam Tuominen, hitherto an unknown name, has won a place among the very élite of our literature; it is a long time since we have witnessed such an important début. What is so strange is that the author who is now making her appearance is a truly original talent. She is an artist in soul and spirit and not merely a more or less good writer...It is certain that she touches the nerve of our time very intimately and that her short stories are no products of literature, but really do contain within their form the living word.

Over nearly twenty-five years Mirjam Tuominen developed an active career as a writer, publishing about twenty books. She wrote short stories, essays and poems. She reviewed contemporary books and translated literary texts into Swedish, among others Rilke's letters and *Die Sonette an Orpheus*. She compiled an extensive biography of Hölderlin. She left two large unpublished manuscripts, diaries, hundreds of pencil drawings and about fifty abstract paintings.

After Mirjam Tuominen's death in 1967 her work fell into oblivion. During the last decade it has, however, undergone a sudden renaissance. Ghita Barck's biography, *Boken om Mirjam* (The Book about Mirjam) appeared in 1983. Tuominen's Finland-Swedish publisher Söderströms Co. published a selection of her work in three volumes, appearing in 1989, 1990 and 1991. In 1992 the firm WSOY published an extensive volume containing many of her most important writings translated into Finnish by Harry Forsblom. Many of her poems have been translated into English by David

McDuff and have been published in international literary magazines. In 1990 her paintings were exhibited for the first time in the Amos Anderson Museum in Helsinki. In the summer of 1994 *Tidig tvekan* was published in a Norwegian series of modern classics. The new coming of Mirjam Tuominen has been hailed by critics in Finland and Sweden. In both countries a large number of articles about it have appeared in the press and in literary and arts magazines. She is also a focus of interest for literary research. It is obvious that this new interest is more than merely the due attention paid to an unjustly neglected author.

By her own Finland-Swedish minority Mirjam Tuominen was until recently considered to be a minor classic, mainly as a skilled short story writer. The Mirjam Tuominen who is now being discovered by new readers and art-lovers, and by a new generation of critics and researchers, is an unfamiliar and surprisingly topical writer. Her development proceeds from traditional prose forms, through avant-gardist poetry and painting to Roman-Catholic mysticism.

The first choice

Hagar Olsson points out that there is an element of choice built into each story in the collection *Tidig tvekan*:

> Each one of these stories illuminates in its own way a certain psychological situation, in which the protagonist, under the pressure of dangerous and contradictory elements in his or her life, has to make a choice.

The most difficult and important choice in *Tidig tvekan* is that faced by Irina in the very first story.

The girl Irina, one of Mirjam Tuominen's many alter egos, is a shy, contemplative, sickly child who has lost her father in early years. Irina has been taken to hospital and hovers between life and death. She sees her struggle as a matter of choice – between life and death, between darkness and life. Paradoxically, it is death that is light, while life is darkness and anguish:

> If one looked towards death, one looked towards the light, but if one looked towards life, one looked into the tangled darkness of a primeval forest. Irina did not want to look into life, it hurt her physically inside; when now and then she made the attempt, the compress began to tighten around her chest, she lost her breath, there was a sudden and unpleasant stabbing in her back. The mere attempt to look into life made one lose one's breath. When one looked into the light for a long time one lost one's breath, too, but in a different way, for another reason: it was

because the light spread within and around oneself, because the clarity grew inside oneself, because one was close to bursting. In life one lost one's breath because the darkness was narrow and full of insoluble contradictions and mysteries, it was narrow and at the same time bewildering large. Irina told herself that she wanted to die.

Irina is the first and fundamental dissident in Mirjam Tuominen's writings. She is different, because she experiences anguish in the face of life even in its most prosaic, everyday manifestations. Life is night and fear, but it is also the daily inability to be like everyone else. In the hospital her *Lebensangst* takes concrete form in self-ironic, nightmarish memories of gym lessons at school and of her inability to 'keep in step with the others'.

Irina chooses life and the anguish of life. She chooses the awareness that her dead father was possibly the only person she ever kept in step with. She comes to the conclusion that 'one should always look ahead, only ahead.'

The absolute

Mirjam Tuominen's next collection of short stories, *Murar* (Walls), was published the following year, in 1939. The first story in this book, *Anna Sten*, is both strange and magical, and thematically enigmatic.

Anna Sten does not possess the thematic elements which, though skilfully concealed, can be traced in many of Mirjam Tuominen's stories, for example *Irina* and *Brevet* (The Letter) in the first collection, and later on *Flickan som blev en växt* (The Girl who Turned into a Plant), *Chérie Klosters dagbok* (Chérie Kloster's Diary), or *Resan* (The Journey). The heroines of these stories are slim, beautiful, intelligent young girls or women struggling on account of their need for intellectual independence on the one hand, and for a physical, "normal" life on the other.

Anna Sten has none of the beauty and creativity of these protagonists. She is totally ugly, totally isolated, totally passive, totally unhappy.

But before Anna Sten becomes the incarnation of absolute misery, she is given a certain number of chances in life. She is gravely handicapped from birth, but she can use her hands and takes a delight in her work as a seamstress. Then her hands are ruined by rheumatism. Anna Sten might possibly have taken pleasure in reading. Infirmity makes her half blind. Anna Sten, who is so repulsively ugly that human beings cannot stand the sight of her, gains the affection of a kitten. The cat disappears. Gradually but inexorably, Anna Sten is stripped of everything. She becomes the sum-total of suffering:

11

She looked as though she had never done anything but suffer and she looked like one who has never reconciled herself in her suffering, who is completely helpless before it. One might have taken her for suffering personified. That was why her appearance frequently had the effect of a violent insult brutally thrown to the face. It was as though she deliberately wanted to force upon people the assertion, for the suffering consciousness at least an atrocious and wounding one, that suffering is completely without purpose or meaning.

What other people find particularly shocking about Anna Sten's face is its expression of active suffering:

It looked as though it had constantly placed its hopes on this earth. Otherwise it would not have looked so desperate. Otherwise it would not have borne this imprint of suffering, of dissatisfaction with suffering.

To the young man Sven Kolmar, who is mortally ill, Anna Sten is as the pawnbroker is to Raskolnikov in Dostoyevsky's *Crime and Punishment*: something that ought to be eliminated. The reason for this is that Anna Sten, unlike Sven Kolmar, still paradoxically, senselessly, hopes for something. But when he comes to Anna Sten in order to kill her, it is she who discloses life's inner essence to him:

And then Sven Kolmar understood that he had forgotten or overlooked the most important thing, he had forgotten love, human love and the one that exists outside human beings; more patient, stronger, more merciless, more compassionate than any human love, because it will not give up until it has forced to the surface that within man that will help him to help himself, life's love for all creation, which for its part will not give up until man has blessed it.

In *Anna Sten* Mirjam Tuominen expounds the essence of Christianity in its most naked and for many its most unacceptable form. She returns to the New Testament and its injunction to love the ugly, the poor and the suffering.

Anna Sten is a timeless story. Its image of suffering and existence makes it possible to understand why, for example, Grünewald's paintings of Christ are so repulsively ugly. Mirjam Tuominen also anticipates Samuel Beckett's terrifying and humorous descriptions of beings that possess nothing except life.

Mirjam Tuominen's Fiction

I have concentrated on two of Mirjam Tuominen's earliest short stories in order to indicate something that characterises all her writing from the very beginning: a continuous research into life's inner essence, a deep penetration into the nerve of life. Perhaps this is what Hagar Olsson had in mind when she characterised Mirjam Tuominen's earliest short stories as 'no products of literature', but as things that 'contain within their form the living word.' During the 1940s the two early books were followed by a steady flow of short stories and essays: *Visshet* (Certainty, 1942), *Mörka gudar* (Dark Gods, 1944), *Kris* (Crisis, 1946), *Besk brygd* (Bitter Brew, 1947), *Bliva ingen* (Become No One, 1949), *Stadier* (Stages, 1949). Shortly after the outbreak of the Winter War Mirjam Tuominen had entered into an impulsive marriage, typical of those days, with Torsten Korsström, the man she had loved for several years. Since before the outbreak of war Torsten Korsström had obtained an art teaching post at the Teachers' Training College in Nykarleby, Ostrobothnia, his young wife had to spend the war years there, isolated in Finland's smallest town, far from her family, her friends and the intellectual circles of Helsingfors. Their daughter Kyra was born in 1941, their daughter Tuva in 1946. For most of that time Mirjam Tuominen's husband was fighting at the front line. Contact was kept up through letters and short, intense visits.

This biographical background permeates the stories of the 40s. She depicts love between man and woman with all that it involves of eroticism, tenderness, struggle for power, jealousy. She depicts childbirth and the mysterious closeness between baby and mother. She depicts the small town and the Ostrobothnian plain. She depicts the war and the alarming upsurge of Nazi sympathies in the Finland of her day.

In routine literary contexts it was often pointed out that in her short stories Mirjam Tuominen specialised in describing children, animals, women and sick people. She certainly described and analysed all these beings with great psychological acuity, but it cannot be emphasised enough that at the same time she gave a picture of the whole society of that time. Through the deviant, who precisely because they stand slightly outside are particularly sensitive, Mirjam Tuominen registers the normal. Through the child she sees the adult; through the animal, human beings; through the sick she describes the healthy; through the woman, the man.

One of her most fascinating short stories is called *Bara en hund* (Only a Dog, from *Walls*, 1939). It is the long monologue of a dog, like many of Mirjam Tuominen's characters struggling to choose between its desire for independence and its need for love. At the same time the dog is witnessing his master's and mistress's painful divorce. The most obvious dissident and outsider in human society is the witch ('Jan and Marietta', from *Certainty*, 1942). Mirjam Tuominen was to return to this subject later on in her poetry, making it clear that her witches are consumed not only by the pyres lit by society but also by an inner, ineluctable fire.

In the book that can be considered her farewell to the short story, *Bliva ingen* (Become No One, 1949) she summarises and anticipates all her themes within one short tale, called *In Absurdum*. It tells the story of a dancer who strives for absolute skill in her dancing and for absolute solitude in her life, who falls and badly injures herself, and who sees God as she is dying.

Victim and Tormentor

> This morning I saw my book: Bitter Brew. In this dawn without light, in which white glowed: melting snow, dirty white walls of houses. Rain, snow, slush, black trees with torture-twisted trunks. December dawn in this city, which can only inspire me with agony.
>
> On this border I apprehend everything painfully clearly. But the tension at my throat gives me the evidence that it is the borderline that, overstepped, leads to the terrain of madness.

The long essay *Besk brygd* (Bitter Brew, 1947) marks a watershed in Mirjam Tuominen's writing, and it has been viewed by many critics as her most important book.

The mood of *Besk brygd* is one of departure and disintegration. Mirjam Tuominen will soon abandon the short story and fiction as literary genres. She is about to leave the small town, and her marriage. Humanity has gone morally bankrupt; the holocaust of Hitler's Germany has been revealed to its whole extent:

> If I were to stand on a square and howl out the horror that has seized me, they would take hold of me and cart me off to a mental hospital. They would look after me and declare me insane, but no one would look after my horror. Because I feel my horror so strongly that I must howl in order to obtain an answer, I am considered insane, but if I conceal my horror in my heart and talk about the weather, the shortage of food, clothes and tobacco, I receive a many-worded and many-voiced reply, and am considered sensible.

Mirjam Tuominen does not howl out her horror in the streets. Instead, she uses the tool she has, literature, to bring order to the chaos and decay. She analyses human guilt and the part played by the tormentor, methodically, step by step. Her starting point is a news item about a German soldier who threw a little Jewish boy into a sewer because the boy cried as the soldier was whipping the child's mother.

This scene remained in Mirjam Tuominen's mind forever. She would return to it over and over again. When she was writing *Besk brygd*, she believed that she could analyse it away or, more typically of her character, that she could take the guilt upon herself.

> I want to incorporate myself into this German soldier, into his body and his soul. I would like to return with him into his mother's womb, be born with him, grow up with him and then, organically coalesced with him, exist until the day when he took the boy and threw him into the sewer.
>
> That is my most fervent wish and and my greatest desire. Often. But I cannot do it, and therefore I am helpless. I know nothing.

In her autobiographical book from the war years, *La Douleur* (Pain, 1985), the French author Marguerite Duras makes a similar effort to analyse a tormentor. She states: 'His stupidity is impenetrable. It is completely without holes.'

In *Besk brygd*, Mirjam Tuominen describes a more nuanced, but equally impenetrable tormentor:

> Yes, if the tormentor could express himself – then nearly everything would be gained. Only he could fix on a pin this harmful human insect – only he sees through it. But the tormentor never speaks, he is the most laconic being that was ever created. He forces his victims to do the talking, the wailing, the stammering – he himself is silent – one might think it was stupidity, but it is not stupidity, one might think that it was contempt for words, but he does not despise words, he is interested in words. It is perhaps quite simply inability. He is bound to the action, the victim is bound to the word.

The classic example of the tormentor who compels his victim to talk incessantly is, of course, the Sultan and Sheherezade in *The Arabian Nights*. Mirjam Tuominen points out that *Besk brygd* could equally as well have been entitled *Sheherezade and the Sultan*. The book's cover illustration is a pen and ink drawing by Mirjam Tuominen's husband. It represents the sensual, cruel face of a man behind the slim silhouette of a young woman.

> The relationship between man and woman is often based on ties reminiscent of those between victim and tormentor.
> We all have a tormentor inside us, we are tormentors to our nearest and dearest, to our children, to animals, to ourselves.

But, Mirjam Tuominen argues, there are people who have both a tormentor and a victim inside themselves. These human beings have a highly developed sense of humour.

> The tormentor has no sense of humour, he is always deadly earnest. How could he have a sense of humour, as he does not speak, but act. There is in fact in every action something irresistibly absurd. The victim senses the absurdity and acts very reluctantly.

15

Mirjam Tuominen constructs a system of guilt and non-guilt, of tormentors and victims. The least guilty beings are infants and animals. This book of meditation on humanity's greatest crime is about 'feelings of gratitude towards a fly, remorse for offence done to a cat, and the genuine joy the company of two infants has given me.' The world of adults is false and hostile to life.

> The infant and the animal love what they see and feel in man, the adult person loves what he wishes to love.
> What makes social relationships with other adults so difficult is that the other person for the most part seems to be indicating that he is associating with someone different from whom one really is, and that one is probably acting in the same way oneself...
> An invisible tormentor, not joy and happiness, seems to be the host at every social event.

Mirjam Tuominen is looking for better company than that hosted by the invisible tormentor. She finds her new intellectual friends among those who, according to her own interpretation, have 'pointed out' the tormentor; writers and artists who seem to have known all there is to know about the problems of guilt and the anguish that 'fill my days and nights until it seems to me that I have sunk into a burning sea of fire'.

Prototypes

Besk brygd concludes with essays on Edith Södergran, Franz Kafka and Hjalmar Bergman. 1949 saw the publication of her essay collection *Stadier* (Stages), which contains studies of, among others, Valéry, Proust, Rilke and Cora Sandel. Mirjam Tuominen was an assiduous reader of literature in the Nordic languages, in German, French, and to some extent Spanish and Italian. She had extraordinary literary intuition and, while she still wrote reviews in newspapers, she often introduced new names. She was one of the first people in Finland to write about Kafka; she was drawn to Hölderlin years before he was rediscovered by literary fashion. But she never treated literature as a source of news items. The essays in *Besk brygd* and *Stadier* indicate that she wrote only about writers she liked and felt spiritually related to.

She writes about Kafka:

> This latterday relative of Jesus of Nazareth was born in Prague and grew up in an incurably bourgeois home.
> One may wonder if there is anything so immensely liable to have a hostile effect, an effect that is deeply and inwardly incurable to the

bottom of the soul, on a growing poetic force that senses its possibilities but as yet has no idea of its own existence, than the helplessly arch-bourgeois mentality.

Franz Kafka became for Mirjam Tuominen an almost ideal object of identification. Both of them are victims and outsiders. They feel surrounded by despotic tormentors who want to reshape and adapt them to "normal", bourgeois life. They both have the harshest tormentor within themselves.

> Franz Kafka had an extremely harsh tormentor within. He was harsh with himself, exacting as to the quality of what he wrote, and equally exacting of other people.

In her Kafka essay, Mirjam Tuominen consciously or unconsciously defines herself and her writings. When she describes Kafka's irony, it is her own sense of humour she portrays, that of the physically passive, non-aggressive victim.

Both Kafka's and Mirjam Tuominen's irony are predominant in her analysis of *Die Verwandlung* (Metamorphosis). The metamorphosis is the only way of escaping the strains of normality:

> Gregor Samsa persists in his existence as a beetle, he cannot part from this existence even by his own will, he lives in his dark, untidy bedroom, shabby and neglected, bitter and ashamed, guilty and yet neither ashamed nor guilty, because if he looks like a beetle in the eyes of the family, then there is nothing to be done about it all, then he must be a beetle, he wants to be a beetle, he has no wish to be the respected son, the good brother any more.

Mirjam Tuominen concludes: 'In order to write a story like *Die Verwandlung* Kafka must have felt the conflict between the demands of his inner being and those of the world around him with extreme and almost intolerable intensity.' She could hardly have found a more accurate definition of herself and many of her own characters.

Two of the most enjoyable essays in *Stadier* are about the letters of Proust and Strindberg. Proust was one of Mirjam Tuominen's constant companions and she read the volumes containing his letters over and over again. Her description of Proust is characterised by the tender irony she used when writing or talking about her literary favourites. Proust was just another of those unpractical victims who make themselves hopelessly absurd whenever they undertake something.

> His letters are as a rule very considerate, so considerate that they may seem to consist of nothing but politeness, flattery, almost. He is so polite that his politeness sometimes kills itself and becomes an impoliteness, because his equally great need for sincerity gets in the way. The result is an intricate arabesque with a succession of constantly new explanations, each of which annihilates the last.

Strindberg was one of the authors whom Mirjam Tuominen read intensely for a while and then later repudiated.

She describes in her essay, not without irony this time, too, the restless Strindberg who included the whole world in his private life and then suffered from having it there, who could not live without women and then suffered from being at their mercy. She writes with perspicacity about Strindberg's paranoia:

> He could renounce neither woman nor the world...Subsequently mankind appeared to him as divided into two halves, one containing enemies, and another people who were not yet his enemies...
>
> To Strindberg, Sweden was Little Puddleton, and anything else one would not have expected, it gave him paranoia, and that is very understandable, even if one might have wished that his brain had retained the upper hand.

It is worth noting that a large number of Mirjam Tuominen's prototypes were men: mostly unusual, "unmanly" men like Kafka, Proust, Rilke or Hölderlin. What preoccupied her, just as it would preoccupy the French psychoanalyst Julia Kristeva decades later, was not the problem of masculine and feminine but that of marginality and dissidence.

Women artists who fascinated Mirjam Tuominen included, for example, the Finland-Swedish poet Edith Södergran, the Norwegian novelist Cora Sandel, the French philosopher Simone Weil, and the Finland-Swedish artist Helene Schjerfbeck. These women, like her male favourites, are characterised by the vulnerability of marginal beings. They are all in pursuit of the same self-consuming search for the the absolute.

Mirjam Tuominen writes about Cora Sandel:

> This writing is in the highest degree feminine, as feminine as Strindberg's is masculine, it constitutes an index of features that are normally feminine, raised to an intensified and therefore abnormal level of emotion in the same way as Strindberg in his writing becomes an index of the normally masculine at an extremely heightened level of emotion. I have never seen a portrait of Cora Sandel and I have no idea what she looked like, but something of the same terrifying, at once defenceless and strong, expression that is reflected in Helene Schjerfbeck's self-portraits emanates from her writings; a white face with dark, wide-open eyes, the expression of a being mercilessly incorporated into the nerve of life's essence and with the same mercilessness exposed to the conditions of reality; extreme sensitivity and extreme, overpowering temperament are here united, the fruit is extreme shyness, a scream of existential agony.

Break and Departure

Mirjam Tuominen left Nykarleby, at first for short periods, and then finally for good.

'The decisive thing had now happened,' she writes in a short prose piece called *Skilsmässa* (Divorce) in the book *Tema med variationer* (Theme with Variations, 1952). 'They were separated, spiritually and physically irreconcilable – and what divided them was stronger than reason and will, stronger than instincts and desires.'

What caused the divorce was not only masculine jealousy at the woman's 'fornication with spirits, demons and non-personified men' which Mirjam Tuominen describes in *Skilsmässa*. It was perhaps above all the jealous, all-consuming attention she herself paid to her spirits and demons. She demanded her solitude and her integrity. At the same time she was torn apart by her own demons.

She lived for a while with her mother and sisters in her old home in Helsingfors – an old, dark apartment, similar to the one in which her little heroines Irina and Magdalena live. A couple of years later, as a single mother, she was allotted a municipal apartment in Kottby, a suburb of Helsingfors. She moved there with her two daughters and lived there until she died.

The book of prose sketches *Tema med variationer* reflects this new phase in Mirjam Tuominen's life. Stories such as 'The New Houses' or 'Ahti Laughs' derive their origin from the new environment: a row of recently and badly built tenement houses, filled with large working-class families, gypsies, alcoholics, social cases and rootless people from all over postwar Finland.

This apartment was the first that Mirjam Tuominen felt to be entirely her own. It was with a feeling of triumph that she sat down in front of her typewriter in the early morning hours. Outside her window building workers climbed on scaffolds. All around new houses were going up. There was a kind of pioneering spirit in the air.

> *Kaveri – kamrat – toveri*: they shouted in the pouring autumn rain, in thirty degrees of frost, Then one had a sense that it was not *they*, these fellows well wrapped up and yet lightly clad: young and old – who were carrying out the work, But that it was angels, While the men – old and young – stayed at home in order to drink hot milk – *Kaveri – kamrat – toveri*: in a long line at 7 in the morning they came. They laughed. They whistled. And did the work: Together. In broken Swedish, in broken Finnish, natural Finnish, natural Swedish, natural Yiddish – homeless from Karelia, homeless from Hangö, homeless from some concentration camp in Central Europe...

With *Tema med variationer* Mirjam Tuominen embarked upon a linguistic experiment, on the border between prose and prose poetry. While hitherto she had employed a timelessly classical literary language, now she strove for the mental leaps of the stream of consciousness.

She was on the way from prose to poetry.

The Poems

> Down in straight lines the birds
> silent O silent
> down down
> into an earth that opens like a sea
> into a sea you plunge.
> Up up.
>
> It closes.

In her first collection of poems *Under jorden sjönk* (Under the Earth Sank, 1954) Mirjam Tuominen abandons the attempt to surround her investigation of the inner world with fictive descriptions of the outer. The characters and milieus of her short stories give way to expressions of the pure self, the idea, silence and a now clearly-enunciated awareness of God:

> Make me pure
> teach me silence
> make me whole
> teach me new words
> words that are not words
> words that are as silence
> whole pure
> not self-abandonment
> not accusation
> not defence
> not thesis
> not antithesis
> but synthesis.
>
> May life and death
> hold each other in balance.

At the same time she herself crosses the border between illness and health, abnormality and normality which she has described many times in her books. She is no longer a sensitive but objective witness who can give reports from both sides. She gradually retreats into a clear-sighted privacy of her own, an isolation that is sometimes very frightening:

20

There is a cry in the forest:
I want to go home
the keys have fallen
the paths have disappeared
I cannot get there
I am badly frightened
I have frightened myself very very badly
they have frightened
I have frightened
I want to go home to the dolls there at home
home to the stove the fire the hearth.

The collection *Monokord* (Monochord) appeared in the same year as *Under jorden sjönk*. It was followed by *Dikter III* (Poems III, 1956), *Vid gaitans* (By the Gaeta, 1957), and *I tunga hängen mognar bären* (The berries ripen in heavy clusters, 1959). For a short period in the mid-fifties Mirjam Tuominen was unable to write and started to draw instead. Some of her pencil drawings were published in *Dikter III*.

The period without words was provoked by two short confinements in mental hospital. This happened against Mirjam Tuominen's will and she interpreted it as an act of deceit on the part of her relatives. She forbade her mother, sisters, ex-husband and most of her friends to have any contact at all with her or her daughters.

Mirjam Tuominen's attitude to society during the later period of her life could be described with the words she herself used about Strindberg's paranoia: it implied a division into two halves, one consisting of enemies and the other of future enemies. She gradually isolated herself from the rest of the world. Her life became the 'work illness poverty' she had anticipated in *Under jorden sjönk*.

She allowed herself only the company of those spiritual companions she loved and trusted: angels, saints, her dead father and a varying number of dead writers, artists and philosophers:

Freud

You who do not want to believe
you have never looked into your brains
I have looked into my brain
I have looked into a shaft
I have burrowed in a mine.
Forty years I burrowed
Moses in the desert in a mine
half a human lifetime
until I got there
A trauma lifted
a pressure vanished

I was inside the vein
brilliant gold flowed out.
Half a human lifetime
in order to get there.
I am in the subconscious.
Another half
in order to will the pure.
My patience is long
as the prophet's in the desert.
A cry comes from mountain peaks:
'I am a stranger
in a land that is not mine.'
I am making it mine.
I will only be content
with the best
the best in man.
Sediment is not water.
I will only be content with water
clear fresh from the primordial source.

But she could not ban the demons, the devils and the tormentors
from her inner world. She chose solitude, silence and light, but
she also received a chorus of evil voices from Hell. She was never
able to free herself from her inner visions of the war and the con-
centration camps. It was precisely those visions that may have
caused her illness. She developed a frightening and self-destructive
ability to react directly and actively to political news from outside.
The atomic bomb, the Korean War, the execution of the Rosenbergs
disturbed her particularly. But even those visions of horror were
turned into poetry:

but the child followed the ball's fate
was carried on women's backs   in gypsy bundles   mass migrations
was gassed beaten to death   kicked
hurled into sewers
thrown from burning houses
by desperate homeless mothers
German Polish Jewish Russian
now without distinction
doomed for racial impurity
never found any refuge
other than cloacas' nether world
there mothers were glad
if sometimes a washroom was opened for them
dirty as in the bistros of southern seaports
with a lavatory hole in the floor
and a device with a grating
for the washing of the inner sexual parts
here they could relieve their bowels or bear the child
which an unknown father of unknown nationality had given them

while they slept unconscious of anything
but dreams of home and gentle stars
and tranquillity's narrow sickle-moon on deep blue late autumn nights...

A Biography of Love

Mirjam Tuominen's last secular 'pointers' were Rilke and Hölderlin. She published a large volume of her translations of Rilke's letters in 1957 and in the same year the first complete Swedish translation of *Die Sonette an Orpheus.*

'Whoever has begun to read Hölderlin will return to him and will gradually become a willing captive of his poetry,' she writes in her introduction to *Hölderlin: En inre biografi* (Hölderlin: An Inner Biography, 1960).

She had herself been for many years a willing captive of both Hölderlin's poetry and his life, which bore many resemblances to her own. Hölderlin's loss of his father, his hesitation between his need for contact and his unwillingness to lead a social life, his brilliant career as a poet, his illness and labelling as an unfortunate and madman – all these drew Mirjam Tuominen to an identification and idealising admiration.

As a biographer of Hölderlin, Mirjam Tuominen reveals equal amounts of understanding and intellectual blindness. There is none of the slightly ironical distance from which she considered Kafka and Proust. Her study of Hölderlin has the intensity and the subjectivity with which one looks at one's child or beloved.

The biography is in fact just as much about herself as it is about Hölderlin. She defends all the phases in Hölderlin's life, and the same time in her own. She even exalts the long, silent period in the poet's life into something inevitable and sacred.

> Hölderlin, with his incommunicable but resigned duty to live for a long time, silent and silenced, without illusions, alone with the wandering clouds, the birds flying outside his window and the minute insights of quietism in his inner being is an inviolable phenomenon. The silence that emanates from the latter half of his life has self-mastery and piety.

God Is Present

In *Under jorden sjönk* Mirjam Tuominen makes Spinoza deduce God's existence:

Out of simplicity
into multiplicity
composed of simplicity
through simplicity
deduced from simplicity
leading to multiple
            simplicity
again leading onward
to new multiplicity
simple deductions
conclusions
all the way to the most
            simple thing of all
the simplest simplicity
arch-simple:
(god!)
the whole.

When in the mid-fifties Mirjam Tuominen began to take an interest in the Roman Catholic church, she entered a more varied spiritual context than the Lutheran church had been able to offer her. The Virgin Mary added motherliness and femininity to the image of the divine. There was ample choice of spiritual company to be found among the saints. Mirjam Tuominen chose Theresa of Avila, John of the Cross and Thérèse of Lisieux.

She converted to Roman Catholicism in 1963 and religion dominated the rest of her life entirely. Her poetry took the form of prophecies and revelations. Her prose turned into a dynamic, often questioning dialogue with the Bible and the writings of the saints.

The book of meditation *Gud är närvarande* (God Is Present, 1961) is the last book she published. Her publisher rejected two subsequent and very large manuscripts of religious poetry: *Jesus Kristus lyra* (The Lyre of Jesus Christ) and *Ave Maria*. Her own sketches for covers for her last published books were also rejected. Her crayon drawings, including the covers, have been recognised as outstanding and exceptional works of art more than twenty years after her death.

Mirjam Tuominen interpreted these rejections as a last unforgivable insult from the outside world. She considered herself condemned to a silence which she had not chosen herself and which was not, like that of Hölderlin, dictated by God.

Her last, silent years, until she died from a cerebral haemorrhage, in the summer of 1967, were possibly the most unhappy period of her life. Writing had been her life, the life she had chosen. Writing had given her human dignity and the strength to 'look ahead, always ahead', like Irina in her very first short story.

I lived my life observing. What I met with, I observed. I was a zero and pure observation.
In the days after I died, however, I made myself very articulate. People wondered why. With good reason. For it was not I, but my observations, that made themselves articulate in a strangely profound, though swiftly transient manner. They flew away and came back again. They fly away and come back again. They named them with my name, honoured them unpretentiously, and it was the unknown in themselves they so honoured.

(Epitaph for a zero. *Gud är närvarande*)

TUVA KORSSTRÖM

FROM **EARLY DOUBT**
(1938)

The Lost Notes

Seven-year-old Magdalena was hopping along the sunny street at an uneven pace. In her hand she held two shiny brand-new one mark notes. Now and then she stopped in order to look at them. She felt immeasurably rich. How many wonderful things they could provide her with. She could not really decide what she ought to choose. One mark's worth of coloured scrapbook pictures, one mark's worth of sweets – or perhaps better, pictures and transfers – or perhaps even better, transfers and sweets – or best of all, just pictures – or what about just sweets? She stopped at the window of the nearest grocer's shop to look at the row of sweet-jars on display. For one mark she could have a large paper bag of white cream caramels, she could also have four cream caramels, but the white ones were probably better, they lasted longer, she could offer them to others, she would be able to offer Mamma one...

Mamma – something suddenly stuck in Magdalena's throat, she lowered her head, forgot about looking in the window and stared down at the pavement. The notes she was holding felt as though they had turned into live coals. Mamma – what a peculiar night she had been through. Never had she known that a night could be so boundless, so strange, and, when she looked back on it – so dreadful. Papa – Papa – something pressed itself heavily together round Magdalena's heart – yes, it had been about Papa, not Mamma. Mamma was still the same Mamma, but Papa, loved, worshipped, passionately admired Papa...Magdalena took a few steps back and looked down at the notes again – they looked back at her in shining self-complacency and haughty unconcern – and suddenly she knew that she loathed them, loathed them so much that they burned her hands.

What if she were to buy sweets with them and let someone else eat the sweets? Yet again she turned hesitantly towards the window. Then she threw herself into a violent run. At the open crossroads, where the wind blew more strongly than elsewhere, she had for a moment to curtail her steps. She opened the palms of her hands and looked at the notes again. They met her gaze with the same haughty indifference as before. Now she knew that not only did she loathe them – she *hated* them. At the same instant the wind seized hold of them and they flew back along the sunny street. She stood still and watched them fly away. Now one of them flew into the gutter, while the other still continued along the pavement.

She could very easily go and get them back. She did not think of it. She thought: 'What a pity, I've lost them! I've lost my money that I got from Papa. What will Mamma say? She's sure to give me a row.'

She thought with regret of the unbought pictures and sweets. She almost felt sorry for herself for having lost so much money. Now the other note too had disappeared. Gripped by a sense of liberation and relief she raised her hands laughing in the air as though she wanted to give her applause to an invisible drama, raised one leg, hopped ten paces on one leg, changed feet and hopped ten paces on the other, took the rest of the way to the door at a run and then slowly went up the stairs.

'Mamma,' Magdalena burst out as soon as she saw her mother. 'Mamma.' She was almost breathless with haste to get the confession over with as quickly as possible. 'I've lost...'

She fell silent in fear, and looked at her mother. – How tactless she was. She had quite forgotten. Mamma could not be treated like an ordinary person today. She had to be approached at a distance, respectfully as one approaches a higher being or cautiously as one approaches someone who is ill, one must treat Mamma with infinite caution today. At the same time as great suffering set her on a pedestal above other mortals, it made her so sensitive and vulnerable that Magdalena almost felt as though they they had swapped roles and that today she was mother to Mamma. She wrinkled her eyebrows and wondered: how could she best put her words? They must begin, she said to herself, almost like a whisper so that they would not rouse Mamma too brusquely to an awareness of her surroundings, they must be spoken in the softest possible voice and chosen so that she would not think about the fact that she, Magdalena, had been present last night, that she had seen – and lastly they must also be ordinary and relaxed in an everyday sort of way so that she would not notice that Magdalena remembered it.

Mamma looked a bit tired. But on the whole she seemed strangely unconcerned, and if one did not know one would have said that she looked as she usually did.

'What have you done then, Magdalena?' she asked in a voice that also seemed to contain nothing more remarkable than a small amount of tired irritability. It was, moreover, a voice that Magdalena knew rather well, it had almost come into being for her sake, for those times when Mamma was getting ready to give her a reprimand.

This strange unconcern made the matter even more difficult in a way. Something began to stick in her throat. 'I've lost...' she stammered out, '...the money,' she concluded helplessly.

Magdalena's mother gave a start of slightly pained surprise. 'The money,' she repeated. 'What money do you mean?'

Magdalena stuttered on the words. 'The money,' she repeated, still more helplessly. 'That money, you know – the mon...' and her voice broke off again. How could she explain, when it was impossible to get either the word 'Papa' or the word 'night' over her lips?

'Do you mean the money Papa gave you last night?' Mamma then said quietly.

Magdalena gave a violent start. How nonchalantly Mamma had spoken the dreaded words! Just as though nothing had happened, just as though it were a question of ordinary money. Just as though Papa had not done anything. Just as though the incredible and dreadful thing had not happened. Just as though the strange, desolate, terrible night that had been had not been at all or had been a night like any other. Just as though it had all been a question of the same old familiar Papa. Just as though Papa still really existed. Just as though...

'But Magdalena, how could you be so careless,' Mamma began to scold. 'What will Papa say?...'

She literally gasped for breath. 'What will Papa say?' Was Mamma mad? Or had she herself, after all, dreamt the whole thing? Perhaps it had only been a bad dream? – she was already inwardly brightening up, but then she remembered the money; that she could not have dreamt. 'What will Papa...' How could Mamma...As though it were a matter of taking Papa into account. As though it were not a matter of complete indifference what he thought and felt.

But Mamma continued and now Magdalena began to be quite certain that she at least still existed as the same old familiar Mamma. The events of last night had not broken her down to a ruin, as Magdalena had feared.

'That was inexcusably careless of you, Magdalena,' she said. 'What will become of you? You take care of neither your clothes nor your belongings. You've a hole in your stocking again, haven't you? And what do you suppose Papa will think when he sees that all you can do with what he gives you is to throw it away in the street?'

'It wasn't my fault,' Magdalena said, in a lame attempt at self-defence. 'I lost them...The wi-wind took them,' she forced out laboriously, until she noticed that her voice was failing her. She suddenly felt so strangely alone and abandoned. She almost felt sorrier for herself than for Mamma. Mamma understood, but she herself understood nothing any more, nothing at all. It occurred to her that she wanted to do something to prove to Mamma how much she liked her, but she did not even know what that something was, only that it existed as something completely futile and superfluous. Neither did she know any more whether she had lost her money or thrown it away, whether she had dreamt last night or really experienced it. And even had she known, she would still not have understood any of it. Suddenly she made a crosswise about turn and ran into the nursery.

'Magdalena,' she heard Mamma call after her, 'it's not done to slam doors like that. Come back at once!'

But she did not come back. She sat down on the floor in the corner by the window, closed her eyes and began to ponder. Had she dreamt it or not? She must make an effort to see it all before her again, right from the moment yesterday when she had fallen ill. She must go throught it point by point in order to be sure she was not adding things that were possibly only an invention of her dreams or her imagination.

It had been at about three o'clock that she began to see the spot in her eyes that announced that the sick feeling was going to come. She had been sitting in the sandpit out in the yard with Kaj when it began. They had been playing the pebble game. 'What are you blinking so terribly for?' Kaj had asked. 'Oh, it's nothing,' Magdalena had replied. She hoped it was the strong sunlight that was making her see the spot. She was blinking in order to see if it would go away or not. It did not go away. She glanced at Kaj's face. It seemed white and far away and she could see only one half of his face at a time. In order to be quite sure, she directed her gaze elsewhere. The white spot grew bigger and followed along, it positioned itself on the white creepers that grew up the wall, it positioned itself wherever she turned her gaze. – So it was true, true and inevitable. Soon a stinging and burning would start in her eyes, then they would begin to ache, then she would start to feel sick and not be able to be sick, then she would be sick, then the headache would begin and then she would wake up in the morning, her face and scalp stiff and rigid. And it was only a week ago since last time! And every night she had prayed to God that it should not ever happen again.

She sighed in heavy resignation, opened her hand and let the pebbles slip down on to the ground.

'But where are you going, Magdalena? Aren't you going to stay out any more?' Kaj shouted after her.

'No, I'm going home,' she replied, indistinctly; it was as much as she could do to steer her way so she could see it clearly before her.

She felt so teeth-clenchingly bitter that she did not even bother to tell Lise, who opened the door to her, about her not feeling well. She crept into the room she shared with Paula and took the cover off the bed. Paula was at school. She would not be home until about five o'clock today. That was good, by then she would be over the worst of it.

She settled down in bed with one hand as a protective shield over her eyes. Now all she could do was wait. After a while she had to sit up again in order to look around her, blinking. Perhaps she had been wrong, perhaps she had only imagined it, perhaps God had heard her, after all.

But God had not heard her. The room danced indistinctly before her eyes in a white mist with scattered black and green spots. That ugly green colour that hurt and made one want to be sick.

She closed her eyes and settled down again. She knew it. God never heard her. It was quite useless even to make the effort to pray to him. But perhaps it was just as well that he did not hear her, since then she for her part would not need to try to be good, as she had promised him she would be if he would help her to escape this illness. She even felt calmer this way. She could turn up her nose at God the way he turned up his nose at her. Since she was as in-different to him as a stone on the ground she need be no more afraid of him than a stone on the ground was afraid. I turn up my nose at you, God, she said slowly inside herself in order to prove how little she feared him, and it was as though the air around her tremblingly gasped for breath, but she herself felt her soul filled by a great, exalted contempt. She promised herself not to ask him for forgiveness when it began in earnest, not to say: Dear God, let it pass, never to speak to God ever again. And, she concluded her argument just to be on the safe side, and again it was as though the air and the objects in the room took one step forward in order to attest that they had heard her words, even if I ask you for forgiveness, God, you mustn't take it seriously, it will only be because I am so ill.

And then it had gradually begun in earnest. And then, just as she had known she would, she had none the less asked God for forgiveness. And when, half-standing, half-kneeling, she had clung to the water-pipe beside the W.C. during vain attempts to completely empty the contents of her stomach, she had also half-sobbed: 'God, dear God, if only you would help me just this once!'

Everything had followed its ritual course. When Paula came

home at about half-past five she had been able to watch her with a pair of eyes that now saw with a horrible sharpness and clarity, it was as though the hammering pain behind them helped them to see even more clearly. But still she had not been sick. Paula had looked at her in that way that always made her heart overflow with a violent feeling of sisterly devotion and made her forget that their life together was a life full of quarrels and arguments.

At the moment Mamma came in through the front door she had at last been sick for the first time.

But here a gap opened in her memory. For after this the outer world had become a world of jumble and confusion that announced itself only intermittently and piecemeal. Never before had the headache reached such a terrible pitch. 'My head is burning,' she moaned. 'It's God, he's punishing me!' she shouted after that. 'Where is Papa?' she also remembered asking. From that she also concluded that Papa had not been home for dinner.

Gradually she had realised that it was no longer God but Jehovah who was punishing her. Only the Jews' Jehovah could wreak his vengeance in such a terrible way. He had sent a lightning-bolt from his sword into her head and now it was seething in there, making the sparks come out through her eyes.

'It's Jehovah, Mamma, it's Jehovah,' she had whispered, without being sure whether her mother was really in the room or whether it only seemed to her that way.

Then the only bright point of the day had arrived. She had been so happy that the the headache had almost stopped for a while and she came close to blessing the moment that had allowed the illness to come over her. Mamma had said: 'We'll move her bed into our room for tonight.'

A sense of great adventure with a smell of Christmas and holidays drifted for a moment past her consciousness. Yes, it was even more wonderful than Christmas and holidays: she was to be allowed to sleep in Papa's and Mamma's room.

She barely had time to sense the world around her changing into a safe and fearless world, before she fell asleep. Now and then she woke up, but only to confirm, half-dreaming, that the power of God's vengeance was somehow paralysed in this room, it was as though Mamma's closeness made her inaccessible to it, shielded her. Was it possible that Mamma was stronger than God himself, she found herself wondering. And she fell asleep again.

Until suddenly in the middle of the night she sat up wide-awake in her bed.

The electric light had been switched on. Only now did she realise that Papa had until now been absent from the room. It was strange that she had not missed him before now, she who had always been more anxious for Papa's company than for Mamma's. But why was Papa behaving in such a funny way? He was staggering this way and that, as though he could neither walk nor stand.

Magdalena transferred her gaze to Mamma and suddenly her heart began to beat as though thousands of tiny, furious hammers had set it in motion. How angry Mamma looked! How angry, and at the same time how dejected and sad. And there was something else, too, something that Magdalena could not quite define.

Papa was speaking in a funny, monotonous, high-pitched voice. She could not make out what he was saying, nor the things that Mamma said in reply, either. All she could understand was that they were quarrelling, almost as she and Paula did, except that it sounded a thousand times more ugly coming from Mamma's and Papa's mouths. Or so she thought, at least, for she had never heard herself and Paula. She made up her mind never to quarrel with Paula again, now that she knew what it sounded like.

She sat cold with horror, listening to the sound of Mamma's and Papa's voices. Then it happened...Magdalena gave a start where she sat in her corner on the floor just as she had done yesterday, and suddenly she realised that it was not some bad dream she had had, but that it must have been real: Papa had raised his hand and hit Mamma.

It was true: Papa had hit Mamma! And the heavens had not come crashing down. The world had not collapsed. Nothing of importance had happened. Nothing at all. Everything had continued as before.

For a long time Magdalena had not had the courage to look at either Papa or Mamma. Now she sat bolt upright, staring convulsively at the floor. She heard Mamma say: 'Can't you see that Magdalena's here? You know how sensitive she is. The doctor said we must be careful with her. Even if you don't have any respect for me, I think you might at least think of her a bit.'

Then Papa had come over to her bed. She felt his hand touch her head. 'Little Magdalena,' he said. 'My little girl.'

She went on sitting motionless, as if she had been turned to stone. The square of floor to which her gaze clung grew and grew, seemed to assume immeasurable proportions. Papa's voice had been thick, as if it were full of tears. She realised it had been like that because he wanted to tell her he liked her, because it seemed to be brimful with emotion. But for some reason her loathing concentrated itself on what he had done to his voice. Why could he not just speak in his ordinary voice? She hated that tender voice even more than the high-pitched one in which he had spoken to Mamma a moment ago. And why did he turn to her and talk kindly to her, when it was Mamma he ought to get down on his knees to and ask for forgiveness? It was, it too, like an insult to Mamma. It was as though he were trying to make her an accomplice in what he had done.

Little by little she had made herself lift her gaze as far as the buttons on Papa's coat. She saw his hands fumbling in its pockets. The two brand-new notes were put on the table beside her bed. Again she felt how she hated the presence of those notes. If they had not existed she would in spite of everything have been able to believe that she had dreamt the whole thing.

'Now you must sleep, Magdalena,' Mamma had said. She lay down obediently. Mamma put the covers over her. The light was turned off. She fell asleep again almost instantly.

The rustle of the newspaper being unfolded reached Magdalena's corner in the nursery through the half-open door.

Her heart stopped beating. All round her it grew deathly still. The rustle of the newsprint gradually filled her ears with a booming sound, filled the whole house, it seemed to her. It was as though everything else was holding its breath just to listen to it.

Papa was at home. Of course he was at home. It would soon be lunch time, and he was always at home then. But today it came like an unexpected flash of lightning: Papa is at home! She had never thought of that. She had never thought she would meet Papa today as on any other day. Indeed, when she thought about it she had imagined that the most natural thing would be for him to stay away from home today and all the other days that were to come.

But now he was at home, quite close to her, in the next room. If it had been an ordinary day she would long ago have leapt up, crept on tiptoe over to Papa's chair, stood behind his back, put her hands over his eyes and asked him to guess who it was. And then he would have turned round, gripped her around the waist, swung her up in the air, she would have curled up in a corner of the chair and they would have read the newspaper together.

Today there could be no question of anything like that. She wondered how she would ever pluck up the courage to so much as look at Papa today. She was so ashamed that it almost felt as though it were she and not he who was the guilty one.

After a while she had at any rate to get up, and with hesitant steps go into the living-room. She stopped in the doorway. Papa did not seem to have noticed her arrival. He sat with his temples propped in one hand and looked at the newspaper without turning its pages any more. But suddenly he said: 'Magdalena, are you there?' And then with a deep sigh: 'Oh, Magdalena mia, if you only knew what a headache your Papa has.'

She wrinkled her eyebrows in distaste. What did it have to do with her if he had a headache? It served him right. It was God's punishment.

'God's punishment.' The words passed through her with a faint start. Why, God had punished her yesterday. Today it was Papa's turn.

Reluctantly she slid down from the windowsill and went into the dining-room, where Mamma stood arranging flowers in a vase. She stood for a moment in silence, watching her at work. Then she said hesitantly: 'Mamma, Papa has a headache.'

'Yes, I know,' Mamma replied. 'He needs a powder. I've got one here. Please go in and give it to him. Take a glass of water with you.'

This was really too much, she thought. Must they all run around looking after him? As though it was he who needed to be protected, as though it was he who had been insulted, as though it was he they must be doubly and thrice-doubly kind to. No!

She put her hands behind her back and looked at her mother defiantly.

'No, Mamma, she said with a note in her voice that was almost one of reproach. 'I don't want to. He can get his powder for himself.'

'But Magdalena, what is the matter with you? How can you be so naughty? Now you will do exactly as I say. Do you remember how we all had to look after you yesterday, when you were ill? And by the way, did you remember to ask Papa for forgiveness?'

Magdalena sank into a deep brooding, which her mother allowed to pass undisturbed. The emotions had again begun to well up in conflicting directions within her. Mamma had said that she was to ask for forgiveness. What for? For having lost the money. After what had happened during the night that seemed like such a pitiful little crime that she could not even try to take it seriously. Mamma was becoming more and more mysterious. A slow indignation began to grow inside her. She thought that Mamma was if anything be-having even more shamefully than Papa had done last night. Her behaviour was so incomprehensible that it set the whole world reeling. Even more than that, she thought it turned the world around her into a world in which she did not know if she really wanted to live. Could one live in a world in which something as horrible as what had happened last night could in the morning be forgiven, cancelled out and forgotten as though it had never happened? It was as though they wanted to force her to believe that the horrible thing was something natural and commonplace, something so natural and commonplace that it was not even worth wasting words on it.

But on the other hand there was the headache. Papa was ill. God was punishing him. Perhaps that was precisely what Mamma was relying on. Perhaps Mamma felt only compassion. Perhaps she had also once known how cruelly God's anger can strike. How strange, were they all now suddenly subject to God's vengeance? Was she herself still subject to it? When it came right down to it, she could not yet have received God's forgiveness, for...Magdalena gave an inward start and nearly turned pale in the face from excitement, for now she felt that she was finally approaching a solution to the problem. God must not have forgiven her yet. He was still punishing her; what if it were her he was still punishing, so that everything that happened was part of the same vengeance he had begun to mete out to her yesterday? Had she not warned him not to take her prayers for forgiveness seriously? Had she not defied him, had she not challenged him, had she not expressly asked him to show his power over her?

Yes, that was what it was. It was she herself whom God was punishing. How strange she had not realised that long ago! But now she understood that it quite simply could not be any different.

That was why Mamma had been so annoyed with her today, quite plainly much more annoyed with her than she ever was with Papa. That was also natural: for it was really she, and not Papa, who had hit Mamma.

Her guilt settled on her in all its weight like a great block of iron.

She threw a long, timid look at Mamma. Now she understood why last night Papa, instead of asking Mamma for forgiveness, had turned to her, Magdalena, and begun to talk to her in a friendly way. Those words had been meant for Mamma through her. When one had done something so dreadful, one could not even ask the person to whom one had done it for forgiveness. It seemed far too inadequate.

But was it really possible to ask someone like Mamma for forgiveness? She was far too high up. Almost like God, she knew everything. Even now she had known everything all along. Known that it was her, Magdalena's fault, all of it, known that it was because of her, Magdalena, that Papa had been compelled to hit her himself. And now she also knew that Papa had a headache, merely because God had not yet punished Magdalena sufficiently, because she had not yet realised that it was at her the punishment was aimed.

Seen in this light, how easy to understand it all became. Now she also understood how right Mamma had been when she had told her to ask Papa for forgiveness. And why in the morning she had talked about him as though it were he and not she who was the insulted and the injured one. How terrible it must feel to do against one's will what he had done last night. Yes, she really understood now – it was worse to feel like the one who had struck the blow than like the one who had received it.

Magdalena no longer tried to meet Mamma's gaze. Now that she understood, she thought it must be brimful of contempt. As brimful as her own heart was of trembling admiration.

Silently she took the tumbler and the powder and took them in to Papa. When he looked up, a sense of relief and liberation flooded through her and she realised that not only had the tangled web that had formed between them been cleared away, but everything had returned to its old, familiar routine. It was as though she had seen Papa again after a long separation, which only made him seem more worthy of love and admiration. But when he made a motion to lift her up into his chair, she felt a violent stab of conscience and she wondered if he would ever be able to forgive her if he knew that she had gone around and seriously believed that he had hit Mamma. She gave him a quick hug, whispered a hurried and half-stifled 'Forgive me' into the lobe of his ear and fled back to her corner in the nursery.

After all, God was still there.

She felt that God's countenance was waiting for her and that it was before this that she now must stand. When it came right down it, it was all something that could only be settled between her and God. But how could she make God see that she really was sorry, that she really was asking him for forgiveness, so he would not need to go on remembering what she had said about not taking her prayers seriously. Above all that he would never again need to punish her by for her sake punishing others. Even the headache and sick feeling were better.

She tried out all the introductions she could think of. She ended up in a regular sweat of anxiety. The right words would not come.

She felt the whole of her insides twist together in a rigid, laced-up, unreleased and heavy sobbing. But God stubbornly turned his countenance away, stubbornly clōsed his ears. She was knocking at barred gates. She thought she had knocked for so long that she must look at her hands to see if blood was not already oozing from them.

And then, suddenly, it came. And she felt that everything around her bathed in a wonderful, deep and silent peace.

All she said was: 'Thank you, dear God, that the fault was mine – that the whole fault was solely mine.'

After a moment or two she added: 'What I mean is: forgive me!'

And after another moment or two: 'Dear God, let the fault always be mine.'

She did not know if she had received forgiveness. She did not care to know it. She did not even care about receiving it. That was not what it was about. That was not what was important.

She knew that now she could safely go on living again. The evil did not exist outside her. The evil was something that existed only inside her. Perhaps she herself was the evil. Perhaps she bore within her all the evil in the world. But around her the world was a peaceful and a good world.

FROM **BITTER BREW**
(1947)

Victim and Tormentor

This morning I saw my book: *Bitter Brew*. In this dawn without light, in which white glowed: melting snow, dirty white walls of houses. Rain, snow, slush, black trees with torture-twisted trunks. December dawn in this city, which can only inspire me with agony.

On this border I apprehend everything painfully clearly. But the tension at my throat gives me the evidence that it is the border-line that, overstepped, leads to the terrain of madness.

But I have been here before.

As a child I was afraid of being buried alive.

The sand pressed into my mouth, into my nostrils, stopped up the organs of breathing.

A Russian photograph from the war. It was hung up in the Helsinki Art Gallery a few years ago. The Jew was already almost completely buried in the ground, only his head still stuck up, around him stood laughing Aryans. They were resting on their spades, pointing their fingers: how ridiculous was this big lonely head above the ground, how ridiculous was this human helplessness, which in a few minutes would no longer be visible, but be completed in the soil.

The victim knew that it is not from the tormentors that mercy comes.

And yet there was a glimmer in the midst of the total helplessness the brown, doglike, trusting eyes expressed: this cruel game must stop. I know children, I have children of my own – where and if they still exist. I know the impulse that amuses naughty children. When they have buried me, they will dig me up again. And only then will they laugh. Only then will it really break out.

But they did not dig him up.

And there was a Jewish boy who ran weeping out to the tor-mentors who were whipping his mother. The tormentors stood in a ring and whipped women in the ring, for they were Jewish women – victim-women.

The boy ran out weeping and shouted: mummy, mummy! for he was seven years old and his mother was still inside his ego-consciousness, and every blow from the whip struck the boy's tender flesh.

Then one of the tormentors turned round – a young man with blond hair and blue eyes of the kind that are called true-hearted –

and he seized the boy by his thin,brown neck – for he was impatient at being disturbed in his task – for a moment he held the boy there, unsure of how to get rid of the burden; then he caught sight of a sewer at the end of the street, ran to it, lifted the lid with a kick of his boot-clad foot, and freed himself of the weeping boy with the black eyes, let the lid slam shut again. A flood of refuse and excrement silenced this child's grief, blinded its eyes, walled up its eyes so that it could no longer see its mother's wretchedness. With a proud gesture the tormentor raised his whip.

Victim and tormentor – tormentor and victim. Was the tormentor created without a voice? Is it only the victim who can express – ? The tormentor speaks through actions, the victim wails in words. What kind of words – ? Helpless words –. The tormentor understands only cruel, harsh stories, the tormentor cannot survive except by means of the very bitterest of bitter brews.

I should like to enter inside this German soldier, into his body and into his soul. I should like to go back with him into his mother's womb, be born with him, grow up with him and then, organically united with him, exist until the day that he seized the boy and threw him down the sewer.

That is my most fervent wish and my greatest desire. Often.

But I cannot do it, and therefore I am helpless. I know nothing.

The worst of it is that no one who uses words, the ability to enter in and imagine, can do this. Fellow-feeling did not exist for the child-tormentor, other people's experiences of pain and pleasure did not exist, he was deficient, he lacked the compulsion to experience in sympathy, he lacked imagination. That is why he is so intolerably inaccessible.

But the same man was perhaps an excellent father to his own children.

Yes, if the tormentor could express himself – then nearly everything would be gained. Only he could fix on a pin this harmful human insect – only he see through it. But the tormentor never speaks, he is the most laconic being that was ever created. He makes his victims do the talking, the wailing, the stammering – he himself is silent – one might think it was stupidity, but it is not stupidity, one might think that it was contempt for words, but he does not despise words, he is interested in words. It is perhaps quite simply inability. He is bound to the action, the victim is bound to the word.

It says so little: 'lacked power of imagination, felt no compulsion to experience in sympathy'. Why did he become like that? What made him like that? What experiences? What tormentor?

The tormentor forces his victim to his knees. The victim stammers, begs. The tormentor jeers, makes the lash whistle. Not for this did I spare you. It is not humility that amuses me. It is your suffering that amuses me. Let me enjoy it in its finest nuances! If you bore me, I will make the process short.

You, reader, who are at this moment closing my book with a shrug of your shoulders and setting it aside in order to return to your daily newspaper – do not do it, it is precisely for you, precisely to you that I speak – it is you that this all about. You have a tormentor inside you just as I do, and if your tormentor does not threaten you with death, so much the worse, perhaps – you look at your child, who is crawling in his playpen. You see that everything here is joy, trust – here at last is the point in existence where the eye may rest and derive belief that everything is good from the beginning. But that was also how the Germans thought, the Estonians, the Latvians, the Poles, when they looked at their children. Yet they took dark-eyed Jewish children, yet they took this trust, infinitely satisfied with its helplessness, in their arms and suffocated it.

We are tormentors in relation to the animals.

I once had a cat – a graceful little creature with long fur, a black tail and a narrow face animated by a pair of large, black, shiny eyes. I became this creature's passive tormentor because I was not able to show it the same tenderness, since I had had a child that usurped the feelings I had previously given to the cat.

Cats are usually self-sufficient creatures that are independent of man. In that case my cat was an exception, but perhaps he was not an exception, either – perhaps it is simply true that cats are proud. But Rasmus, my cat, was also humble, he begged for tenderness, he appealed for human contact. When he was no longer granted this kind of contact, he directed his feelings elsewhere – to other cats. He made a friend – a tom-cat like himself, white like he was, but without the black spot on his tail and with blue, blind eyes.

This blind, white cat became an active tormentor for Rasmus. A strange cat-contact, a tormentor-victim-contact replaced in Rasmus's life the human contact that had been severed by the birth of my child, which for Rasmus meant that human tenderness collapsed, disappeared, and made an incomprehensible, harsh, empty atmosphere arise. With all the hidden, distorted lust for power that can characterise a crippled animal, that blind cat dominated Rasmus.

And Rasmus underwent a gradual but thorough transformation. He had been a happy, trustful, inquisitive little creature, fond of adventures and pranks; he became a soul-sick, brooding, shy, gloomily split cat, whose inner disharmony found direct outward expression in his appearance, which became neglected, dirty, wretched in the highest degree, Never did he approach his food plate until his blind friend had turned up and eaten his share, the best and biggest one, and as thanks the guest would give the host a hard blow with its paw and disappear or give him more of a thrashing. With that bewitched emotional fixation that characterises the victim's attitude to the tormentor, Rasmus would sit for hours waiting for his tyrannical friend. All his movements were marked by tortured suffering, but it is impossible to say what this suffering consisted of deep inside – whether it was fear, hope, frustrated longing, love or loathing. – And when one saw them side by side – Rasmus, graceful, handsome, still indescribably charming even in his decline, with his wonderful, clever, living eyes, which, to be sure, now reflected illness rather than clarity – and the other one: clumsy, repulsive, ugly, swollen with inner sadism.

Thus did Rasmus live the dismal and intense existence of a creature-victim, until a dose of rat poison ended his short, tragic life story. It happened when I was away on a journey, and I must always think that he chose to die a few days before I returned, a few days before the return of his human tormentor.

It is not fear that spellbinds the victim to the tormentor.

It is a bewitchment of another kind, caused by other peculiarities – peculiarities that must exist in the tormentor. The victim wants to learn to see through the tormentor. But the tormentor cannot be seen through – sadism is not transparent – the victim can never comprehend his tormentor, and if he does, then he is no longer a victim and the tormentor is no longer a tormentor.

The subject 'animal and man' would appear in this respect to be inexhaustible. From the animals' point of view, man is the Nazi. From the animals' point of view, Nazism was the high-point of organised humanity. All Nazism's apparent inventions: gas chambers, sterilisation, castration, reckless experiments with living beings, were old inventions or inventions that were already there – they had all been tried out on animals. The capon that is castrated and placed in a narrow basket to be force-fed with a funnel is only one small example. As an animal in relation to man, I would want to eradicate everything human within me. How good everything would be, if only man would disappear. If only man's organised, self-important, self-preoccupied sadism would disappear. How everything would live and breathe, liberated.

Johan Ludvig Runeberg, that man who has been half written to death, suddenly came alive for me one day. I happened to read an anecdote about him and the anecdote was quoted in a newspaper column, not in order to throw light on Runeberg, his life or his poetry or his love affairs, but in order to illustrate the grammatical errors that occur in the traditional presentation of the anecdote.

During the last two years of his life, Runeberg – so the anecdote said – kept company with only two beings, and those beings were a mouse and a fly. It is possible that I remember wrongly, that the company consisted of a spider and a mouse or a fly and a spider, but whichever of those small creatures it was, it does not strictly speaking matter in the present context. The main thing was that it dawned on me that Runeberg was a very living person, a person whom it would have been impossible not to like.

Without any pretensions I can in this instance compare myself to Runeberg. For almost a year my only company consisted of a baby and a fly. The baby is scarcely comparable to the mouse – considered as company, a baby has no rival among all created beings – but the fly...

If there is one truly repulsive guise in which life has incarnated itself, I suspect that it belongs to the fly. The flies are every bit as repulsive, every bit as nasty, every bit as horrible as Sartre portrayed them in his play *The Flies*.

And yet all this is not true. For if one begins to keep the company of a fly, one may be seized by something that strongly resembles love. At any rate, I almost began to love my fly. I got to know him, he acquired a face for me, he lived with an individual temperament. It never failed to happen that every evening, on the stroke of seven, after I had put my baby down to sleep and thrown myself on a sofa in order to give myself up to reflections caused by the forlornness and desolation of wartime, he turned up, and I am convinced that he turned up solely in order to keep me company, or because he himself needed company. Autumn, winter and spring, every evening at this appointed hour he arrived in such a touchingly loyal manner that my initial irritation was soon replaced by expectancy and semi-gratitude. He was small and delicate as flies are when they survive the winter, and he had something of a dog's trust in his movements as he flew around me in ever narrower circles. At last he landed on my hand and looked at me with his black dots of eyes, and he had the same pained expression on his face as the one a dog can sometimes have, a dog that has been treated like a human being and has gradually for that reason come to the false conclusion that he is a human being: he was tormented, intensely tormented by not being able to express himself, by not being able to speak.

That summer I travelled away, and what became of my fly friend I do not know, but I know that he was one of the few friends I have ever had, and strictly speaking the time I spent with him brought me more benefit than many a human contact.

The dog that is treated like a human being becomes a careless human being, a good human being, in other words – a human being in whom the germ of sadism is lacking. In a world from which human beings had disappeared, one could imagine the dog as man's successor. But unfortunately the dog cannot exist without man. Without his master he is helpless, he goes to pieces or returns to his origins. So strongly fixated is the dog on his master that one may suppose he suffers from this attachment – if the master were a tormentor one could speak of victim-fixation, but this is not usually typical. The dog becomes an emanation of his master's best qualities, for the dog is attracted to the best in man and is touchingly unreceptive to the bad in him.

At any rate, my husband's dog emanates my husband's best qualities, and if I want to talk to my husband, it is really best done by talking to his dog.

All this does not prevent the roles sometimes being reversed. The dog becomes master, and the master becomes dog. In that case the dog is no longer an emanation of his master's best qualities, but of his worst ones.

This strong attachment of the dog to man is in reality repugnant, and it is also the thing that most offends me about dogs.

Reckless subjectivity tends towards objectivity.

This book, written by me, is about myself and I think I shall also dedicate it to myself. Yet – and perhaps precisely because of this – I feel as though in it I were appealing to all the people in the world.

If I were to stand on a square and howl out the horror that has seized me, they would take hold of me and cart me off to a mental hospital. They would look after me and declare me insane, but no one would look after my horror. Because I feel my horror so strongly that I must howl in order to obtain an answer, I am considered insane, but if I conceal my horror in my heart and talk about the weather, the shortage of food, clothes and tobacco, I receive a many-worded and many-voiced reply, and am considered sensible.

If with these eyes of mine I were to see a person split in two, it would not surprise me. Or perhaps it would surprise me, but not if after that I saw a throng of people coming out of him.

When Manja Got Better

One Sunday morning Claude set off for the hospital to see Manja. He felt sorry for Manja.

We always feel sorry for people who love us more than we love them. Our compassion is often mixed with a little contempt. We know ourselves a little, and we cannot help perceiving that it is certainly not we who are the worthy object of such an ardent longing, such a passionate striving. And the greater our compassion, the more overwhelming our contempt, the more hopeless grows the dilemma of the one who loves: ever more ardent the longing, ever more useless the striving. We become less and less capable of obliging, while the other becomes more and more capable of loving precisely us.

Manja had loved Claude. And the more deeply she had loved, the more impossible had it become for him to return this passion, which he had nonetheless kindled in a fickle moment. Manja's love was concealing her real essence. It was asking too much for Claude to love her. He saw an unhappily distorted creature which an evil, monomaniac power had bewitched – this creature he mistook for Manja. She could not awaken his love, and since he possessed no love his imagination felt no impulse to discover the real Manja, the concealed, the hidden, the enchanted.

A person who loves gives herself away charmingly, gracefully, unaffectedly, if her love is requited. But if her love is not requited or requited only in a very small degree, she can rarely appear as anything other than distorted in the beloved's eyes. If her character is proud and reticent, her movements become shy, inhibited, stiff in the beloved's proximity – or they also become too lively, falsely intoxicated. But natural, unaffected they are not, and it is only the beloved who could make them so, and if he does not want to, or is unable to, she who loves must constantly strive to conceal her desire and yet at the same time beg to have it fulfilled; she wants the beloved, but more than the beloved she wants perhaps herself in him, to receive herself back, to regain her free, untouched essence.

Claude had with conscious or semi-conscious intention aroused Manja's passion, because practically any new, comparatively young woman – and Manja was at that time new to Claude – eventually aroused the urge for knowledge within him – and in addition to the urge for knowledge, the need for erotic contact or at least for the certainty that erotic contact was possible. But it was a long step from this cold, erotomaniac need to real love, and Claude would probably have been more careful had he been able to anticipate how all too well he would succeed in Manja's case. He had the erotomaniac's double attitude towards women, an attitude composed of tenderness and contempt, which few women can resist – on Manja its effect was overwhelming, for she needed tenderness, she was a phenomenon that existed in isolation. And even if she could not avoid perceiving the sick contempt and self-contempt that seemed to constitute the very precondition of Claude's tenderness, how greatly she preferred it to other men's total lack of tenderness. She imagined that she saw a Claude whom no one else had seen, she wanted to show him a Manja whom no one else had seen, but Claude, who certainly felt self-contempt, none the less cherished a greater interest in himself than in Manja's Claude, whose existence he was, moreover, able to sense only faintly. It seemed to him that Manja was in the grip of an illusion, it inspired him with contempt, this illusion bore his own features, suggested a Claude he did not want to know about, it filled him with irritation and increased his contempt, but she seemed so agonisingly fettered to this creation that had been conjured up by reality, desire, intuition, imagination and the life of the instincts he had kindled, that she also inspired him with compassion.

This Sunday afternoon Claude was filled with a deeper compassion for Manja than ever before. So deeply, so frighteningly deeply and genuinely was it experienced by him who had really long ago made himself incapable of anything but false emotional states, that his contempt gradually faded away among the depths. He did not know that; and as for the irritation, Manja was no longer able to irritate him, she could not threaten his freedom any more, nor seriously offer him a love for which he had no appetite.

Claude also had one major reason to feel compassion for Manja. Manja was mentally ill and there could be no doubt that it was her unhappy passion for Claude that had caused the illness. For Claude, who was a doctor, there was nothing romantic in the statement of such a fact. He knew that when illness breaks out it often does so in association with erotic experiences or erotic desires. Manja's being had been exposed to a violent shock, neither soul nor body nor soul-body had avoided experiencing the effects; those countless, tiny messengers who circulated in her blood with their important messages, had fallen into reckless confusion, they no longer obeyed orders, did not forward the messages or forwarded them all too eagerly and busily. The result was a tremendous disharmony and disorder: mental abysses opened, an inner chaos, an inner landscape that raged like a volcanic eruption. Manja had to go into hospital for treatment.

Claude had not been in contact with mentally ill people for a long time, not for ten years, since his student days; he had never had an acquaintance, a friend or relative who was mentally ill, he was in other words not really used to people who were mentally ill. But as soon as he entered the hospital waiting room and found himself among these women who were no longer ill enough to need to be kept locked up in the disturbed ward, but were far from being well enough to regain their freedom, he had the same sensation of having entered an enchanted castle, a magnetic tenderness which he now recalled having experienced when young. It was a much deeper enchantment, a much warmer tenderness than the one which he as a gynaecologist felt for women who were ill, and yet after hesitation he had chosen to become a gynaecologist, not a psychiatrist. The diagnosis was so much easier in the former case, good results not so hard to obtain, and women who were ill or in childbirth did not inspire an indifferent anguish, a confusion concerning the self, in the way that the mentally ill ones did, whether he liked it or not. Above all, perhaps: Claude had those hands – gynaecologist's hands. They were impersonal doctor's hands when they performed their work, and Claude never mixed eroticism with the practice of his profession, but when he stood with his gloves on at the examining table he felt something of the same impersonal emotion as a pianist at his piano, and his fingers touched uteruses and ovaries with the same impersonal tenderness with which a pianist touches a piano's keys. His hands felt impersonal sorrow when they touched diseased organs, impersonal joy at the touch of healthy and beautiful ones, and when they discovered a uterus that lay protectively around a fertilised ovum, they felt the joy of creation, excitement, stimulation.

Where did this irresistible charm of the mentally ill come from? Like shy, silent and restless birds in a cage they flitted through the corridors and the waiting room. The wide sleeves of the ugly, grey dressing-gowns fluttered, but the awkward hang of the hospital smocks could not conceal the soft, graceful movements that seemed a matter of course for most of the patients. A quiet mood of expectation, exhilaration hung in the atmosphere – it was visiting time, a feast even for those whom no one ever visited.

There was Manja coming now. But what a Manja – she did not look like the healthy Manja, and yet she moved him in quite a different way than the healthy Manja had done. Her thick chestnut brown hair was uncombed, even looked unwashed, fell in a tangled, matted frizz against her shoulders, her forehead and made her very pale face seem more ill than it perhaps needed to. With an impulsiveness, a cheerfulness he had not encountered in her before, she greeted him: 'Claude. How nice of you – '

He took one of her emaciated transparent hands in his, burst out: 'Manja – ', and suddenly he felt pierced by a new, great tenderness.

But Manja had turned her gaze away. It was as though she were no longer conscious in any way that he was here, with her. With the same impulsiveness, the same almost violent curiosity with which she had looked at him at the first moment, she was now looking at one of the patients.

He wanted to call her attention to him and he repeated, now pressing and appealing: 'Manja – '

It worked. With one of those very swift movements that seemed to designate the ill Manja, she levelled her brown eyes, which had become so deep and shiny, at him and looked into his face, straight into his eyes, eagerly, hectically searching and yet quietly and impassively watching. Then her gaze softened, gave way to compassion. 'You have suffered, Claude,' she said. 'I can see by the way you look that you have suffered.'

He was moved by this deep compassion in a being he had not expected to have room for any suffering other than her own. The great pity he had felt for Manja all day finally gave way to a compassion of quite a different kind. At the same time he noticed – and it was a great surprise – that Manja was right in what she said. It was true, he did suffer, had suffered constantly. For many years he had imagined that he had grown past personal suffering, that he had passed it like an immature, repressed and unenlightened stage of life, and then now, this discovery, that he was suffering, that he always and constantly suffered. It was going too far – and was it dizzying clear-sightedness or catastrophic weakness? Claude wondered whether he too might not be on the way to becoming mentally ill. The whole system of laboriously built-up superiority and unconcern, the whole of this system which he had grown into as into another, an adult nature, was in the process of collapsing, and he felt the flames from a despair that had once burnt him flicker dismally near. He looked at Manja, almost in search of protection. She turned her gaze towards him, but he noticed that the gaze in her eyes was just as intensely directed inwards as, a while back, it had endeavoured to capture impressions in the surrounding world. And he also saw that her eyes seemed to be covered by a film of unshed tears and that the gaze beneath this frozen film seemed dim and broken. This gaze seemed to speak of a suffering borne so intensely that Claude could not bear to watch it for long, but instead began to look at her hands which, narrow and flower-like, rested against the chairback in a peculiarly expressive position, the one clutched hard round the other.

'You're looking at my hands,' she said in her gentle voice, and he was surprised that she still seemed conscious of his presence. 'Yes, I'm holding on to them. That way I have something to hold on to.'

She laughed a small, soft laugh and again plunged her eyes into Claude's eyes with the same inquisitive, eager gaze, and again there began that violent, intense searching in the world of his eyes. Claude let it happen, he opened his eyes to her and he did not feel like a person or an individual, but like some piece of unknown, alien land to a traveller from far away, or like some fragment of a desert island to someone who has been shipwrecked, or like a star to an astronomer. But while in this way he opened himself to her, so that she would be able to examine this piece of a fragmentary and incoherent outer world, he was assailed by a bitter sensation of loneliness, a sense of absolute desertion. Her eyes continued their urgent searching, which was hectic, and penetrating, too, but in a way that was outside the knowledge Claude possessed, they searched not because these were Claude's eyes, but because they were a pair of human eyes in the greatest generality and because they happened to be situated nearest to her field of vision and to constitute a part of this surrounding world which she was as yet only able to apprehend as fragmentarily as an infant, and which piece by piece she must recapture and make into something like a relative whole. Manja's eyes searched in his – Claude's – eyes, it occurred to him, in the same impersonal, uninterested manner as when with his hands he searched in women's sexual parts, not because they belonged to any specific individual, but because they were women's sexual parts in general, areas which he had to examine. And in almost the same way, outside his work, he had loved women. He had loved them because of a need to feel the impersonal tenderness their bosoms radiated in moments of sensual contact and because of a need to get to know the impersonal reflection from their tenderness-thirsting and banal or strange souls that lingered on in their sexual parts and breasts, but without a need to get to know these souls in the way they expressed themselves in other contexts.

But right now when, a second before, Claude had found himself so catastrophically close to a despair that had once been his and was still perhaps his, even though he no longer acknowledged it, but overcompensated for it with more and more eroticism, more and more sense-intoxicated joy of knowledge, more and more contacts, stronger and stronger doses, fresh contact, more knowledge, more and more conscious joy, pleasure controlled and sharpened by the intellect – now he also recognised the endless sense of loneliness that had been connected with this despair that once was his, and all his soul cried out for contact, deeper, more lasting contact than that of the moment; communion, warmer, more secure than and above and beyond the occasional communion of physical contact. What a person he might become in such a communion –

And instinctively, intuitively he appealed to this Manja, whom he knew had loved him so passionately, but also so tenderly, so compassionately, so coolly and unselfishly that each of his least desires had been a law for her. He appealed to her out of that desert of loneliness that had taken him captive. It seemed to him that he could have given his life in order merely to be able to call her to him for a moment, experience a true contact with her, a naked, unreserved, warm contact, a moment of mutual recognition.

But Manja had got up. A new visual impression was attracting her and involuntarily she was moving in its direction. He saw her eyes, how they searched in the stranger's face, just as curiously, eagerly and just as impersonally as before in his own countenance. Then he experienced the whole of that hopeless sense of isolation and humiliation that comes over a person who with his whole being desires to surrender himself to another and is at the same time bitterly conscious that such a surrender would be worthless, that the other person is incapable of accepting it.

He looked at Manja and she seemed to him graceful, beautiful, direct as a child of one year. He felt that he loved her with a tenderness so strong that it hurt him.

Once more he called softly; Manja –

And she turned obediently round, looked at him, was intensely with him, but just as intensely turned away from him, it lasted only a fraction of a minute, then she and her eyes had gone to another area for searching.

And Claude realised that he was no longer Claude, whom Manja had loved and striven for so intensely. She really no longer needed to inspire him with irritation, contempt or compassion. She no longer loved too much, no longer yearned and desired to the point of madness, she had hidden herself behind a veil, she was no longer helplessly abandoned to impressions from her fellow human beings and the surrounding world, but instead she was searching behind a veil, was rendered inaccessible because of it, searching in her own inner world and in the eyes of other people, but herself not able to be reached by them. In certain essential respects Manja resembled a one year-old child – she was not happily newborn but unhappily newborn, she was not happily unconcerned but painfully unconcerned, her growing took place not in a state of rejoicing but in a state of torment, but she was growing none the less – to a new, stronger wisdom.

Claude went. In the doorway he turned round, tried one last time to call Manja to him. But Manja's attention was no longer on him, her gaze slipped indifferently and eagerly past him.

Then Claude felt something like a strong self-pity.

The Child and the Demons

A boy of six had to go dressed in ragged, foul-smelling clothes, his parents had a bad reputation and it was commonly said that the boy had head-lice. He lived in a small town and because of all these reasons, but especially the supposed head-lice – and there is no cause to doubt what is commonly asserted – it was natural that the boy could not find any playmates.

He would sit down in the gutter outside his parents' hovel of a house, and from this vantage-point watch the other children's games. It was clear that he longed to be rid of his isolation. But when some time had passed he seemed more indifferent to it and after some more time it seemed almost broken, not because the child was less excluded than before, but because it seemed he had decided to accept facts. He no longer heeded the playing children, his eyes had acquired an inward-turned look, not indifferent, but intense and concentrated. For those who had an eye for such things it was obvious that the little lice-carrier had weaned himself from the childish, fellow-creaturely world, that he had given up his pretentions of taking part, that he had abandoned himself to his demons, that he had done so with complete devotion and that his demons were consequently more kind than cruel to him. He had entered a strict nursery school, but with every day he deepened in insight and he found that while the demons certainly demand without limit, they also give without limit, and what was more, he found in the demon world a mercy that he had not encountered in the human world, and he surrendered himself with confidence to this mercy.

To the other children of the street it simultaneously and quite quickly seemed to become clear that they did not need to fear the lice-infected child any more – not even the fussiest and socially pliable and most obedient of them reminded him any more that he was there without permission, one who was not allowed to come near and whom one was not allowed to go near.

But gradually another change made itself noticeable in the boy. His gaze was not as it had long been, directed inward in torment and fascinated concentration, but remained as earlier fixed for long moments on the playing children, calmly and clearly observing and evidently unconcerned that the taunts might begin to rain down again.

But perhaps it was the children who threw the taunts who were right. In actual fact during this stage the excluded child practised an art which during the Middle Ages was punished as a mortal sin and designated as magic. He studied the playing children's spirits so that if he needed to he could summon them to him. This took place in intimate harmony with his demons' will, for demons certainly love isolated people, but wish on the other hand to see those whom they love grow in insight and willingly let them have company, just as long as it is not the warm and secure kind, but the cold and abstract, or the swiftly devouring, hot and short-lasting kind.

But that the boy truly gained in wisdom through his study of the child-spirits one could again perceive from he expression in his eyes. They were not timid, hungry and suspicious as they had been before he had surrendered himself to the unknown within him, but neither were they tortured and burned-up as they had been during the first hard time in the strict school, nowadays they often assumed an expression that was open and fearless.

Then one day a wild battle arose among the playing children. One of them had been given a football, and the reason for the quarrel was that they were inexperienced and could not agree on how the football should be used so that they could all join in the game. The excluded boy sat in his usual place in the gutter and observed it all for a while, but when the battle merely increased in violence and when the disorder merely became worse he got up, almost against his will it seemed, imperceptibly he entered the quarrelling crowd and within a few minutes this demons' disciple, who had never played with a football either and had never had a playmate at all, but who possessed his deep knowledge, acquired through patient study, of the quarrelling children's spirits, had brought order to the confusion, calmed the most impetuous, made even the most eager combatant quieten down and set in motion a game in which all joined in and none stood outside. The children seemed never to have merged together in a game to such a degree, and only when it was over did they notice who had been its leader.

Then another dispute arose. Some of the children argued that in future the boy should be allowed to take part in their games, while others argued just as eagerly that he should be chased away and moreover punished for having sneaked his way into their company, and others did not express their opinion but remained neutral.

And the boy himself.

He had taken up his place in the gutter again and did not take part in the discussion. Were one to conjecture from the expression on his face, he was neither pleased nor sad, neither happy nor unhappy, neither proud nor humiliated. Deep inside him meanwhile the dispute resounded and it would probably go on resounding there for a long time: warm, eager voices that spoke for intimacy, cold, hostile voices that mistrusted it and did not even want it, mute voices which with their silence said that it was all the same: for or against. Each 'for' could moreover happen momentarily or apparently only, while 'against' must be the stable and decisive element.

And the silence spoke, as it usually does, with the voice of reason.

But suddenly something happened. No one had ever seen the boy laugh nor even so much as smile before. Now he lit up, grinned openly, broadly and largely, lips, eyes, his whole being took part. The gap left by the recently fallen-out milk teeth in his front jaw also grinned, opened black and without end, inwards.

A milk-tooth grin. It is always wherever it appears a street-urchin's grin, a gutter smile. And in spite of this its effect is slightly moving.

In Absurdum

She was a dancer and she was sad.

As far back as she could remember in her life, and that was from the time she was four, so it had been: dancing and sadness, sadness and dancing.

The sadness isolated her, set her apart. She spoiled everything if she danced in a group. She could only dance solo parts and even they had to be specially chosen. She thought them out herself gradually. All this isolated her even more. She felt inferior among her colleagues – she became like a child separated from them in the midst of a dance. She was allowed to dance solo when they danced in a group, but she could never forget the moment when she became separated. An abyss opened between her and the other children. She thought that they looked at her compassionately, sorrowfully as at one who was sick, one who was dying. She felt she was dying, dark, abandoned, intolerably distressed. But she forgot her sorrow when she saw them dance: it was beautiful, the mutual rhythm, the hands, the limbs, leaves, fluttering plants that bowed as though to the wind. Waves in a mutual sea. No children, no people, music paraphrased in living line patterns.

She was shown the instrument that produced the music she was to dance to: the violin, dark, 'intense, onesided', a recluse. It smiled seriously, could not weep, could not laugh, could only master these states to the point of unbearable tension. It was accordingly the instrument that was deposited in her body. To that music she had to dance: always alone. She felt antipathy, fear, but as towards an unavoidable fate. And when something feels unavoidable one has merely to adapt oneself, that is relatively easy.

And she continued. Dancing and sadness – sadness and dancing. When she was dancing she was only dance and when she was not dancing she was only sad. But out of her sadness grew her dancing, just as the dancing seemed to make her sadness grow. She fought against her sadness with her dancing, but at the same time the dancing increased her sadness and this is no contradiction, for in addition to dancing she had to exist.

She fell in love. She became sadder. Her rhythm, her nerve-covered body's rhythm was in no way like her husband's. She had a child. She was glad. At the same time her sadness increased. She met a man. Was happy. His rhythm was at last her rhythm. The sadness was transformed into a vital joy, dance, lightness, gracefulness. She danced, she loved. She felt that only now was she learning to dance. At last. The natural rhythm in her body released itself. Her dancing became free and controlled. The movements narrower, stricter, purer, more purposeful. She sought out the difficulties. The joy was in overcoming them. The liberated, individual rhythm in her body made dancing as she had danced before too easy for her. She became critical, created problems, sought her way to new unfreedoms, which she fought against, overcame. She combined, calculated, invented new dance numbers, the ideas and the impulses rushed over her.

Her body felt more and more related to the wind, the water, the air – light. At the same time there came times when she noticed that all this was the upper side of a sadness that had grown beyond all limits. And she realised that the stronger life became in her, the more must the pain and the sadness increase.

She separated from the man, whom she had told herself she loved and who had told her he loved her. She did not know why, only that it was necessary. She was no longer weightless with love, she was unfree, heavy. It was no longer life, it was life mixed together with existence.

But the sadness came over her and murdered her will to dance. She was no longer dance and sadness, she was only sadness.

She stopped dancing. She spent the days watching her two year-old child at play, the dance of a fly, a kitten's movements. I cannot reach further than they can, she told herself. They are perfect, I cannot overtake them. Not too much, not too little. The only thing I can strive towards is their degree of perfection. To master consciously, yet in self-forgetfulness, what they master unconsciously, by instinct.

Life or movement, movement is life. The more intense the movement, the more intense the life, the more controlled, the more perfect. And the more suited to its purpose. Dance or movement: the philosopher's idea, the growing tree, the child's play, the fly's dance on the windowpane, the kitten's game with a ball. But the degree of perfection the tree, the fly, the kitten, the child express has not been overtaken by anyone: philosopher, poet, artist, dancer.

She isolated herself – she withdrew in order to live with her child, in order to dance in solitude. Filled with a burning drive for perfection. There were creatures that lived in the Alps, jumping from ledge to ledge. Clumsiness was fatal for them. She wanted to live up on the mountain like the gazelles – they had the most beautiful movements that were encountered anywhere. In addition, to dance for the most complete, most expressive and pure thing that could exist: silence, not the human kind, which was terrifying, because it broke only into dirtiness, but for the childish kind and for the inhuman kind: the silence of the spaces and the mountains.

She was punished for her hubris. She fell, and broke her leg. And, what was more, fell mortally ill.

Pride, madness, people had said about her solitary dancing.

Now they came to her and showed her sympathy and a little I told you so – a great deal of I told you so and a little sympathy.

A dancer with a broken leg. That was a cruel fate, one could not help feeling sorry, even though the dancer had behaved more like a monster than a human being.

But she did not feel sorry for herself. She did not have time, and so she was turned towards non-existence.

She was alien to them. She knew everything about them and nothing about them, just like God. She knew everything about their lives, but she knew nothing about their existences. They existed and she lived. They existed and lived, they mixed them together, but she only lived. Even though existence had sometimes been such that she had starved, yet she had only lived – and considered the other as being like a disturbing but irrelevant dream. She had had no I, no sense of self and she had always regarded herself as the worst. And yet, sometimes when she took a pause in the midst of a violent movement, still, unmoving, rest, waiting, infinite movement in a narrow room, the rejoicing had risen within her: I am I, I am everything. The rest in the dance, which was not rest but imperceptible movement, was the most demanding moment, and it was perhaps it that corresponded to her existence. And if it was not so, it was in the last analysis the state that was closest to life and closest to existence.

I have experienced everything now and now I am experiencing God, she thought, but without arrogance, very humbly; every dying person experiences God.

God was there at the beginning of the world and at the beginning of all things, all people, plants, animals, at the beginning of time. He understood everything, completed his movement and withdrew back to Nirvana. He remains in the movement of all things, because they were originally his, were set in motion by him. But as far as he is concerned the movement is complete, earthly existence does not concern him, he lived and then withdrew back into a form of existence that suited him better: Nirvana. Even if he could see his work he would not weep with distress, it would be impossible because in non-existence there are no tears, no disappointment, no remorse. Pain perhaps, if one could express the concept with a word that corresponded to that of non-existence, but there are no impure, mixed-together concepts. But if he can look back and if he can feel loss, he surely looks with a great sense of loss back to his most perfect creation. First: to the infant with its absurd trust, faith in spite of everything, faith across boundaries, attributes, doubts, hesitation, only faith; then: at the child, who is only life and incapable of lying – of mixing together, in other words. How did it arise, this misunderstanding that governs the world, when the beginning is such? he might ask himself, if he felt like asking himself anything. They ought to begin over again from the beginning before the beginning.

Thus did she think. Very clearly, very definitely and distinctly. Even though her body was really in a condition such that she could not think at all. Broken in pieces, shattered, torn tissues, darkening pain in every nerve, pain that awoke the call: for liberation.

It rained. Streams, floods of rain. Day and night, nights and days. She liked the consciousness of rain. It refreshed. It was the only thing that refreshed. And it made her see: a piece of black spring earth, a bulb in soft soil, and somewhere nearby water.

And the first human being looked at the first flower. In the dawn of creation this happened. She was completely turned towards life. God was still there and had not driven people out into existence.

A woman in the next bed was looking at the flowers on the dancer's table. The woman was a farmer's wife and had surely seen flowers before, but perhaps she had not seen hyacinths, strong, passionate in such a way that everything around them becomes pure; home from a warmer clime. Now she looked at these hyacinths and the dying dancer looked at her eyes: wondering, wide-open, earnest as a child's. Looking for the first time. Completely turned towards life.

Perhaps it had been meaningless. Whatever it was, the sick woman seemed to forget her torments as she saw: become whole.

The dancer closed her eyes.

FROM **THEME WITH VARIATIONS**

(1952)

Death in Muteness

First she was quiet. – Then she said nothing. – But then –
She grew mute. A terror that had always been there suddenly
unfolded. An illness that had imperceptibly grown great, washed
over and through her, a giant wave; it left no nerve unmarked. A
door was slammed violently shut, and secured with heavy locks.
Inside was she. Outside the mute one. Outside her blood, where
the terror burned: a rose with a fully opened interior, outside her
heart, that hard-pressed thing, her limbs, eyes, but far inside her
ears' shells – she was there, the mute one. Grieving foot-soles
fettered her thoughts, staunched her blood, pinioned her hands,
on pointed needles her heart trembled in spasm or writhed under
walls' stone weights, constricted throat sent no air to willingly
gaping lungs.

Like a heron in a cage she died: on guard; entangled in the near;
her eyes caught in the remote; frozen cry to the distance; frozen
cry inward; each tensely quivering, exaggeratedly sensitive nerve –:
Waiting for disaster.

Divorce

The decisive event had now taken place. For so many years she had committed adultery and fornicated with spirits, demons, men not personified but precisely for that reason in his and perhaps also her imagination all the more real. And during all these years he had suffered the hellishly nuanced phases of the fearful illness that goes by the name of jealousy, and which in his case was all the more tormenting since his distrust had no definite object towards which to direct itself. He got up at night in order to catch his wife red-handed, he rolled on the carpet in despair and his fingers crooked in a wild desire to strangle: Nothingness, pure nothingness, but he did her no harm. She on the other hand, who was so shame-less that she behaved shamefully with pure nothingness, and was the cause of such suffering, became more and more like a suspected, though at the same time consentingly loyal, member of a totalitarian state: an accused, who paid heed to her thoughts, dreams and emotions – there was always something worthy of indictment in them. She became more and more strongly convinced that she was commit-ting adultery and that she was deceiving this man who looked at her with eyes that with each day were colder with hatred, more brilliant with new judicial decisions. And had it been possible for a person to reflect the expression in her own eyes, she would have been able to see the look in her eyes after each night deeper with severity, forced to master: antipathy, horror – the longing to escape.

The decisive event took place when it broke out over her lips: thunder-like, exploding – the shriek that was a scarcely audible whisper: leave me in peace. – I don't want you to touch me. There will be a disaster if you do – the world will come to an end, every-thing will burn! – Ohhh – Go away, just go away!

He went, proved to himself and his absent wife that it was only in relation to her that he was paralysed – and when he returned in the morning his eyes were colder with new and quite fresh judicial decisions. The woman he had been with had been repugnant to him and within himself he felt complete revulsion at all the women he would now be forced to approach in order to confirm his liber-ation from his wife.

And as she looked at him, the aversion deepened in her eyes and became night. They were separated, spiritually and physically irreconcilable – and what separated them was stronger than reason and will, stronger than instincts and desires.

But between them ran the child, the chirruping birdsong, unsuspecting, unconcerned. And he felt the difference immensely when she stopped talking to the child in order to talk to him. And she saw the judge disappear and his eyes shine with tenderness, when from her he turned towards the child. They smiled to the same child, and they felt that the same love moved in their hearts. Their gazes met in such simultaneity, and sympathy, pure, unbiased, disinterested, became perceptible in their inner being. When they became conscious of this a vague hope awoke within them. They let the newly-awoken sympathy nose each other's bodies rather as a dog for an initial moment noses a book that has got a fresh food-stain on it. The sympathy nosed, and they felt each other's bodies like two aching corpses.

And the sympathy turned its muzzle away from the corpse-smell.

Travels

I

I came to a land where freedom had been realised or was at least believed to be very close to its full realisation. For the people here the word freedom could consequently not be applicable to themselves but only to other peoples who had not yet discovered the happiness-making formula that means the realisation of freedom. In this land, therefore, the people talked much and with a strong sympathy for all the people beyond the frontiers of their own land who were not free. It was said that one ought to exert oneself to the uttermost in order to liberate all the lands and peoples of the earth. On the other hand, it would hardly have been the right thing if it had occurred to some compatriot to longingly invoke, for example, the concept of freedom in an internal context, to himself or any of his fellow-countrymen. To be sure, it was not forbidden by law to use the word freedom in that last-mentioned way, but a universally sanctioned convention in reality liquidated the word freedom for any contexts other external ones.

Since everything in this land was so new, so thrillingly and inspiringly new, I became like a child, reborn, receptive and avid for knowledge, and also became involved in teaching in a school. By day and by hour I received proof which confirmed that freedom really was being realised in this land as in no other. On the way to work, in buses, trams and underground trains the workers sat studying books which promised them the chance of experiencing freedom completely realised even in their own lifetimes; a mother married to a simple sailor told me with eyes moist from emotion that there was every reason to expect that her son would attain the rank of admiral one day, and everywhere there was testimony to the fact that here women were acknowledged as beings equal to men with all their human rights acknowledged: among other things the fact that within the military profession they possessed the rank of captain, major and even colonel.

In the light of such experiences, the old world I had left behind receded ever further into my consciousness like some primeval night, half-real. Here I had been born anew, here everyone was happy – there was no talk of anything else – and everyone was firmly resolved to save the whole world, against the whole world's will, if necessary. Everyone lived for the mutual welfare of everyone else.

But of course, I could not forget the old world completely, and as is often the case when one tries to repress painful memories, the past returned in my dreams at night.

And I dreamed that I was trying to invoke the word freedom. That merely to suceed in uttering and adducing freedom on my own inner – melancholy, for example – personal behalf would offer me the most nameless solace and happiness. But I could not utter the word, so strong on the other hand, also in the dream, was my conventional awareness: countless inhibitions made the syllables stick in my throat, until, sobbing with anguish, I reached the point where the four letters: f, r, e, e – got over the threshold of my consciousness. I knew they were there, but I did not utter them, I did not even think them.

When I woke up I was soaked through as after the most terrible nightmare.

And I said to myself that this was not suffering but imagined or pretended suffering. But in this dark night my repressed primeval consciousness refuted this assertion and said that it is precisely when we tell ourselves that we are only pretending to suffer that we really do suffer, for why should we acknowledge a suffering about which we can do nothing? The soul is mortally sick – but the soul's suffering is always imagination.

II

Here again the people seemed neither happy nor cheerful – if one judged by their outer appearance. They looked dreadfully tormented, pale and sickly, and indeed the children – viewed with the inexperienced gaze of a stranger – were pure cripples. Instead, it could be said that here the cause was radiant, and there really was no reason to doubt people when they claimed to be happy in the service of the common cause.

Here prejudice was exalted into a religion. It had been said that the old religion had lost its grip on people's minds precisely because it was not prejudiced, but on the other hand it was clear that in the long run people could not live without belief; the belief that there must be something that was exalted above temporal existence was actually just as necessary to them as their daily bread; to proceed from any other hypothesis was to undervalue man – or to overvalue him, whichever way one wishes, but in any case absolutely wrong. Now it was desired to unite the social or the useful with the religious and it had been discovered that it was to society's detriment that man had been created so: with a left eye and a right eye, one hand that spread to the left and another that spread to the right. His inner being tried to conform to the physical, but could only do so in a dilatory, useless and therefore harmful way: what succeeded for the body, so that for example the two eyes saw a single image instead of two, was impossible for the soul and the consequence was dualism, disunion, splitting. Now what was desired here, in contrast to what had always been the case everywhere else, was to proceed not from the outer but from the inner. The physical must be adjusted, and as the basic tenet of the common religion a single saying from the annals of the old, inapplicable religion was borrowed: 'If thy right eye offend thee, pluck it out.' More dogma than that was not really needed, for this one tenet gave rise to a countless number of variants and above all it fostered unity in a way that had hitherto been unknown.

Like people who had acquired an absolute formula for mutual happiness, they gave themselves up to selfless labour for the education of the growing race. To this end they set to work in the way that adults in every country usually do when children and the disciplining of children are involved: the adults pretended to do what the children had to do in earnest.

I visited one of their schools and I shall never forget that visit, such a powerful impression did the whole experience make on me. The teacher was a young man, pale, earnest, with the same tormented expression that seemed to be a part of people's physiognomy here. He wore a thick white bandage round his head, his right hand was in a splint and was held still in a broad, black-gleaming silken sling. After him followed his little disciples, similarly bound up, in exactly the same manner, the only difference being that their bandages concealed real wounds and bodily injuries. They had that same morning had their right arms broken and their right optic nerves sprayed with a poison that had made them blind forever in that eye. But none of them complained, none even moaned, they walked silently and earnestly all the way to their work, which consisted of carrying heavy loads of bricks, and on the left side of their backs one could see the hint of a hump-like protuberance which in time would inevitably grow much larger.

The young teacher fixed his burning dark gaze on me. Quite certainly he saw through me, for agnostic and foreigner unfamiliar with their customs as I was, I could not help watching the small children with growing anxiety. – You see, said the teacher, how happy they are, no adult can serve more selflessly than a child and make sacrifice for the sake of a great goal. When this race has grown up it will be invincible.

Thus did the teacher speak, but as I looked into his eyes, which could in their fanatical misery be called beautiful, there came over me an oppression so immense that never since have I been able to breathe naturally as I could before. I saw that the teacher was right, that these children might perhaps just as well be called happy as unhappy, and I saw for the first time full confirmation of the fact that man is prepared to make any sacrifice at all, just as long as he is assured of the existence of a clearly-defined good and is trained in the years of his youth to serve that good.

The New Houses

Slowly – but then suddenly, very quickly, almost too *dizzyingly* quickly, one thought: The new houses have progressed. Almost with regret one saw the scaffolding disappear around the house-fronts and the white plaster surface exposed: with those blind empty eyes that showed everything was still unfinished inside. One saw: How they handed one another the beautiful red tiles: patiently submissive – politely compliant, beneath Jokes – sorrow: The stones were transported. Were carried further and suddenly the roofs were covered. – With joy one saw the first small green shoot come up among the planks, the gravel, the unfinished things –: that were not needed yet – in the courtyard; the green shoot that became a second, third, fourth green shoot: Among planks, rubbish, remains of the demolished collapsed now unneeded shed – more and more fragments of green were coming up.

Kaveri – kamrat – toveri: they shouted in the pouring autumn rain, in thirty degrees of frost, Then one had a sense that it was not *they*, these fellows well wrapped up and yet lightly clad: young and old – who were carrying out the work, But that it was angels, While the men – old and young – stayed at home in order to drink hot milk – *Kaveri – kamrat – toveri*: in a long line at 7 in the morning they came. They laughed. They whistled. And did the work: Together. In broken Swedish, in broken Finnish, natural Finnish, natural Swedish, natural Yiddish – homeless from Karelia, homeless from Hangö, homeless from some concentration camp in Central Europe – and him: At home here –: From European slave-ragged-lost: – to Communist – to People's Democrat – to Social Democrat – to Swedish People's Party supporter – to Finnish People's Party supporter – it became *edistys*, it Progressed: the tiles were passed across from hand to hand – so that it became *kokoomus* – Coalition and Wholeness. As quickly as possibly they collaborated – with the least possible waste of time, waste of strength.

The first, who did the heaviest work – disappeared to new work that was the heaviest of all – He, the one who pushed the cart: In thirty degrees of frost: He pushed the cart fully loaded with iron: backwards and forwards – forwards and backwards – he pushed it up there on the roof – which did not yet have the beautiful red tiles – And disappeared: Before he was able to see the tiles –: To another cart just as heavy.

Afterwards came those who had the easier work – On which the March, April, May sun shone – Towards the easy it progressed.

Towards the difficult it went to completion: The way that people live.

Requiem

Black terrifyingly Great – Great terrifyingly Black the Smoke suddenly rose up:

above the green carpets of grass, above the hills' soft grass, above the ornate patterns of the gravel paths, above the grass of the hospitals, the grass of the barracks: Rose the smoke Black:

above the water it rose, above the deliberately dancing necks of the swimming ducks, as they stuck their beaks in the water, as they flocked together and held conference, as they separated and floated apart, alone for a while, together again; above the naked bathing laughing children and the grown-up people Rose the smoke, Rose above the gulf and above the sand on the shore – where the tears for once, Did not flow to an end: – above the locked-up bay rose the Smoke, above the locked-up sick people by the bay, above the locked-up promenading sick people in the locked-up garden by the bay Rose the smoke, above the closed-in gardens of the healthy, above the healthy locked-up people: the soldiers in the barracks Rose the smoke:

above the fallen rose the smoke, above the fallen's fallen flowers, above the fallen in another way: the dead too early, fallen too soon: precociously dead, dead too late, fallen too early precociously: dead, Rose the smoke, above the thousands of roses above the fallen, above the millions of flowers above the dead, Rose the smoke:

above the great cross, higher than the great cross: Visible to the ducks, Visible to the naked bathing laughing ones, Visible to the locked-up sick people, Visible to the closed-in healthy people, Visible to the fallen, Visible to the fallen in another way: dead too soon, too early fallen: dead; Visible the cross rose – But higher – Rose the black dense pillar – thunderclouds many combined in union – in towards the sky, in towards the city:

The smoke:

Visible to the angels that kept watch by the graves, visible to the little plump smiling child-angel, Visible to the serious vigilant searching strong one; Visible to the statues and Visible to the granite, the rock and the stones, Rose the smoke:

above those who had living fallen:

on the sand, the rock, the lawns – here and there – they lay like living fallen –: absent eyes absent in a piece of needlework, absent hands absent crocheting softly solitarily pliantly smoothly – absent eyes absent in a book absent hands absently clutching a pen – Gaze at the dog that is dying: Close to it –: it falls dies – by mistake it has taken in a poisonous drug of death and howlingly-pitifully draws its last choked-shrieking breath – or Gaze at the five-year-old child at the polyclinic: Close to it –: after three hours' waiting tearing his hair desperately hysterical, hysterically desperate, all this time no one puts a crayon and piece of paper in his hand – or hearing's Gaze into the rock, the cave: There is weeping there: an abandoned child, an abandoned dog, an abandoned death, an abandoned madman, a homeless cat, wing-covered bird, deep-diving bird's worn-away webbing – or Elsewhere-gazes at men: Close by – who fell living with a store of spirits bottles. Or gaze at the lost old man with ragged gaze wandering in the sky, When he unwraps the greasy paper around his sandwiches – during muted incessant conversation from this side to that – from that side to this – soft quiet staccato-conversation – the soul that is not here, the death that is not there.

Absent lost gaze: Everywhere cemeteries. So many. And all fenced round, enclosed, furnished with barbed wire. All even after death, compelled, forced to keep to their own: Protestant, Jew, Russian, Muslim, Catholic – Swastika, Hitler Youth – agonisingly fallen, doomed to eternal misunderstanding – persecuted to death, killed for persecution.

All sending messages above earth. All still keeping to their own.

Rose the smoke black great wholly terrifying.

Rocking lulling quiet lullabies. Rocking dead people to rest.

Vignettes

From a great darkness not far away: The writer's hands fell nonplussed
and saw the birds wheel in wide, wide circles with obvious wings.
From great darkness in front: the writer's hands fell nonplussed.

And were raised no more
Pinioned fettered
They wailed weary
Languished withered
Faded down.

In beaten palm
There was a throbbing, clamouring, crying
There was an aching beneath skinless skin.
Twisted magic claws growing out at the side.
One eye fell down into the well
Another flew up to heaven.

Deep under the earth sank the ear.

Help was not to be found above earth
All the healing help came from the dead one.

FROM **UNDER THE EARTH SANK**

(1954)

Down

Down in straight lines the birds
silent O silent
down down
into an earth that opens like a sea
into a sea you plunge.
Up up.

It closes.

Make Me Teach Me

Make me pure
teach me silence
make me whole
teach me new words
words that are not words
words that are like silence
whole pure
not self-abandonment
not accusation
not defence
not thesis
not antithesis
but synthesis.

May life and death
hold each other in balance.

Sing

The night is near.
The dark is rising.
It has already risen high.
Sing.
Death is near.

Place counterweight against counterweight
on the scales of life.
The scales of death are full
so steeply is the balance tipped.
Place counterweight against counterweight.
The one so light the other so heavy.
Counterweight against counterweight is needed now.

How easy to be caught in a crevice
to incline sheerly to fall.
To close one's eyes to sleep only sleep
in this embrace as light as air as space
and for always forever.
Forever: O death
dark truth-sayer
implacable
gentle exposer of lies
filth evil.
Take me! Hide me!
Let me sleep!
Infinitely O infinitely
you allow your own to sleep.
Sleep sleep sleep
while the truth works
on their closed eyelids
and resting hands
resting like cut flower-stems.

I had already forgotten
that it would be so easy.
It had already had time to become
new unfamiliar.
It frightened me.

I understood now
that it could be shocking
this violent way
of keeping not only life company
but also, devotedly, death
the reverse side of the medallion
the up- and downturned scale
the one that catches darkness
as wide as oceans and earth
and the heavenly vault
that is stretched over oceans and earth.
And the stars' blindly gazing eyes
and the bloodthirsty moon's
indifferent wishing towards new fullness, new wholeness.
Life and death inseparably united.
Murder and birth
Birth constant birth
and birth too is death
death and life inseparably united
but not mingled together
that is the cycle
that is the moon's blind will
and the blind will of man
and the blind will of all things.

Long enough death's kingdom held you
captive.
Long alas long enough
you sojourned there.
It set you free.
It gave you life
when everything collapsed.

Break the magic circle!
Mingle no more together
death
with life!

Will there not still come days and nights
when the snow falls soft?
Encircle engird fence round!

Can an accuser lower himself
to a marriage with his accused?
What content of joy
could be extracted from such a marriage?
The prosecuter accuses
the accused defends herself.
The accuser pronounces or defers the sentence
the accused lives in taut expectation.
Is that love?
I ask I ask I ask.

One day the bow will be stretched too taut
One day it will have to snap.

From you alone.

Fresh snow will come
fresh white soft snow
stillness goodness work
Work illness poverty
that is the trinity:
life.
Stillness kindness work
which alone and solely signify
work illness poverty
Live for that
that was what met you
when it was happening.

The magic circle is broken
the accused is free
executioner and victim are a construction.
Whoever lets himself be accused
becomes an accused
whoever lets himself be victimised
becomes a victim
whoever lets himself be crucified
becomes a cripple.
And whoever spreads fear
yes, he *spreads* fear.
Better
not to let oneself be accused

not to let oneself be victimised
not to let oneself be crucified crippled
not to spread fear.
The one who wants to prevent fear
exists in fear
and perhaps attains reconciliation.
The one who wants kindness
is neither executioner nor victim
but simple
The one who is appointed executioner
becomes an executioner
if he allows himself to be appointed executioner
the one who is appointed accuser
becomes an accuser
if he lets himself be appointed accuser

But it is not the accusation
(which is perhaps false)
not the defence
(which is always pointless and unnecessary
if the accusation was false)
not the sentence
only the deed that convinces.
Some must die.
On their closed eyelids
their resting hands
resting like cut flowerstems
on the ash the dust of what they were
the truth works
implacably incorruptibly.
Not self-surrender
only unavoidable death
or continued life without self-surrender
is the deed that convinces
sooner or later
later or sooner.

So build life's ship
build it strong
build it with good will
honest desires uprightness
build it

on solid foundations
on death's foundations:
your foundations
on life's:
also yours.

Invocation

Beyond the seven mountains
the seven valleys
the seven rapid torrents
the seventy-seven nights
the seventy-seven days
the seven hundred-and-seventy-seven days-and-nights
the seven thousand and seventy-seven paradise years
inferno years purgatory years
shut up in the mountain
beyond the valleys
beyond the rapids
beyond the nights the days
the days-and-nights
the paradise years
inferno years purgatory years
inside shut in
outside shut out
I cry: Awake!
Come back!
Why did you abandon me?
A whole is more than a half.
A half cannot live as a whole.
Awake awake awake!
Go back the long way
the hard way
over the seven mountains
through the seven long valleys
Soar float plunge
over through
the violent currents
the dangerous whirlpools!
See:
I look like a human being
and am a semblance
a hollow shell
without you.
You say that you are dead.
I say that you are asleep.
I call you back

I cry out for you
I beg I appeal:
come!
The darkness takes me
fear screams
shrilly with a bird's voice.
Fear O fear fear
nothing but fear
you gave me life.
Give me back
set me free
the chains rattle.
I weep
there is blood where I walk.
Fences grilles barriers
the birds are eating from my eyes
those cruel birds with strong beaks
and averted gaze
O birds birds birds
harbingers chosen ones shimmering white deep-black
you
not those cruel ones, not the eagles
but you
mortal harbingers
you that travel with messages from death
take me on your wings
fetch me back
birds birds birds
sorrow-swan black swan lonely swan
I call upon you I cry out I beg
wild swan
you that do not exist
I who do not exist
gentle swan:
Fetch me back
give me back
my living entrails
out there outside
inside shut in!
Give me
grant me
fetch me!

Sorrow-swan black swan
harbinger from death's kingdom
together we must plunge
soar float
the veils of the water are soft
the sky without weight.
It is easy to soar
hard to walk.
Breathe breathe breathe
like the bird
when it floats.
I want to travel the long way
there
return again
here.

Let Go of My Hand

Let go of my hand you idle grasp!
Here no human hand can help
Neither father nor mother.
Neither brother nor sister.
Neither husband nor wife.
Neither doctor's advice
nor doctor's knife.
A child has known what you know.
Do not fear
the fall, the deep one!
Vertigo
only takes the one who is afraid.
Be silent!
Go forward!

Wild Roses

Wild thickets thorn hedges
bar your way
wayless.

But the insight
at the bottom of all our souls
the same: and only.

Our only common inheritance
our only common ground
and bottom in depth of the most extreme necessity.

Amidst thorns and wounds
all at once
fragrant wide-open exhaling.

I Sit Abyss

I sit abyss at your brink.
Only those who have themselves been seized by vertigo
know what fear is.
The child does not break faith.
Nor the one by childlike insight led.
Green-gleaming valley at your brink.

I sit abyss at your brink.
Does not the conscious rise up.
Does not the unconscious sink down.
Peaceful   beautiful   face
you help me.
Deepening valley at your brink.

,

The Rock

You climbed down from your mighty rock.
Looked at me looked at the rock.
'What a beautiful rock,' you said my child.
'What can a rock like that have in it?
Surely it must be something beautiful?'

A rock is a being enchanted
by the earth, child.
It cannot fall deeper
than that earth receives.
But if the earth stops.
If it disintegrates
or fire surges out of its entrails
or a strong quaking a violent shaking
pass through it
then the rock will hurtle falling
down down down
until new earth comes to meet it.

'And what if it hits against something harder than itself?'
Then the rock will split into many small fragments
which all of them each and every one
are the rock and only the rock
that contain nothing but rock.

'And what if no new earth comes?'
Then the rock will fall eternally forever.

Fever Chart

A world a ball of fire
torn loose from its orbit
hurtles through space
hurtles without peace
falls without blessedness
    finds no coolness.
Hurtling hurtling falling
fires through space.

Earth into earthlessness casts out what earth will not acknowledge.

Without peace or rest
restless without peace
peaceless in the land of a thousand lakes
torn in the barbed-wire land of many limits.
A mother-tongue a weight
towers of brick hurtle smother fall
mountains of rock transform rock.
A land where the fathers lived
but they rushed past
abandoned for centuries: stranger
    in the prehistoric land.

But what concern is peace of yours
what concern joy blessedness?
Blessedness was never a concern of yours
you want to go to Inferno
to the people there
you rush you fly
their locks burn in fire
and yet are not consumed
in Inferno the people are pure
pure though without peace
the fire inextinguishable equal.

What is life to you
what is death to you
what is anything to you
what is fever to you
what is tiredness to you?

You are dead.
What is the child to you
what is even the child to you?
Feverish illusions
        the veils of tiredness
they are something to you
they are still something to you.

Give

        child's way of seeing

give

        eyes

joy.

In Inferno the people are pure
like the fire
burning inextinguishable
        and alike

The Cry

There is a cry in the forest:
I want to go home
the keys have fallen
the paths have disappeared
I cannot get there
I am badly frightened
I have frightened myself very very badly
they have frightened
I have frightened
I want to go home to the dolls there at home
home to the stove the fire the hearth.

The Swallows Fly

The swallows fly
high
in towards bluer sky
low
down beneath darkening clouds.

'In the midst of the state'

In the midst of the state of mighty never
in the interior of the mine
one can see what was not seen
hear what was not heard
feel what was not felt:
buried alive.

Burn Witches

Burn witches
witches bewitched ones burn
bewitched in witchery by witchery
taken
witches burn
you guilt's enchanted
burn to death in fire
you who never were
it was in the land of somewhere
you who always were
it was in the land of elswhere
burn burn to death
that which ever was
it was in the land of nowhere
self that seldom was
it was here in this land
all of you burn burn to death!

Narcissus

All your words came to me with another meaning
a sealed meaning.
Beyond your words I sensed your faces.
The faces you bear are not your real ones.
You were disguised masked veiled.
Your unveiled faces are more beautiful
you were all prisoners in the veiled.
You hinted you insinuated you concealed
but all this did not reach its goal
it was stabs in blind scratches in the skin
the real was always much further away
it sometimes reaches us like an echo
it is the game that perpetually must fly.
Who says that Narcissus has been enchanted by his own image?
Whoever it is has never looked into the water.
Few have looked into the water.
Whoever has seen his own face in the mirror of the water
has seen all the others'.
Whoever leans over the water
and perceives his image
will not return, he will vanish.
Your unveiled faces come to me
they are beautiful
unalterable because true
they reach their goal
the truth is always beautiful
redeeming freeing giving.
I am divided from you by a singing stream
you will never reach me again.
From far away sometimes an echo reaches me.

Marcel Proust

You were the slave of your false fancies.
In this paradox such an irony:
your life
the child's struggle to become a man
the man's struggle to renounce being a man
the youth's struggle to remain a youth
to die old
who was more powerful:
the sultan or sickness?
Scheherezade or imagination?
And who was the one
who the other:
one gaze was turned away
another turned towards.
The loving was cruel
the cruel was loving.
Thus is a life motivated
thus is born an idea with variations
without end
Am I different?
Were the others different?
Was anyone different?
The same thing manifests itself differently.
Everywhere prisoners
enchanted
sick.
Everywhere a virgin concealed
(out of the sea she rose
into the sea she fell
ebb and flow)
bewitched
captured by dragons and djinns
pursued even into the secret castle's
most secret interior.
Where now is Françoise the French the fresh
holding the pillar upright?

The Duchess's feet are shod in those brilliant red shoes
when anyone dies
the Duke hurries off to another masked ball
and the haste of the disputatious doctors is stilled.
(Just observe
the nervousness
among the individual animals
the individual plants!)
During solemn speeches
with measured gestures
they give themselves time
prepare the poisoned brew
the brew that initiates
into the last redeeming transformation.
In this paradox
who was more powerful?
The one already condemned to death has fled
a strange object lies there.
The books stand on the shelves.

The sensitive is fleeting and profound
it couples badly
slyly or briefly with the sensual real
it contracts to the touch
grows speechless blind
loses its grip
finds no refuge
withdraws
couples with a mobile clear vision untouched
turned away
(sultan: you were never any concern of mine!)
turned towards
the intellectual
regains
finds connection.

Hamlet

Behind the forehead is the realm of the dreams.
But your forehead bears the seal of peace.

Monologues wonder softly
if life is more than death
if death is more than life
if the two might not be reconciled
they quarrel in the realm of the brain
tear apart the realm of the heart.
You sob are bitter
joke jeer
mock
degrade all that is holy.
Give me back my reason
O lord our king!
Behind the forehead is the realm of dreams
Dreams dream that dreams
dream that dreams that dreams.
Dreaming you dream
to an end
know no way out
no end.
Where is the road
the path
    the pass
out of the dreams?
for dreams only dream
more dreams to dream
dreaming they dream themselves out
know no end
where is the road
the path
    the pass?
here there are only dreams
O lord our existence!
You are just an imagining
yet so despotic
where is the dreams' way out?
when will the dreams come to an end?

O sovereign over life!
O queen death!
Let me out!

The queen is near.
The king by her side.
How were the dreams woven behind your forehead?
Here is the father.
Here is the mother.
There is the child.
The king is near.
The queen at his side.
You do not see them.
Ophelia is married
has children.
Ophelia is already a matron.
You see none of them
You know none of them.
You hear none of them.
You want none of them.
You want to go behind the realm of the forehead.
You want your inner realm.
Behind the forehead is the realm of the dreams.
But your forehead bears the seal of peace.
Where you lean your forehead
in the moon's reversed sign
O Prince of Denmark!
in the moon's transforming radiance
in the pellucid night
there the realm of peace is mirrored.

Descartes

You discovered the meaning of reason
of logic
of consistency
of anti-mysticism
of irreligiosity.

You rushed to the church
you called to the Virgin Mary for protection.
You were logical
you perceived
the consistent.

Spinoza

Out of simplicity
into multiplicity
composed of simplicity
through simplicity
deduced from simplicity
leading to multiple
                    simplicity
again leading onward
to new multiplicity
simple deductions
conclusions
all the way to the most
            simple thing of all
the simplest simplicity
arch-simple:
(god!)
the whole.

Nijinsky

How long after all can a story exist
a poem
and be treated as real?
Unreal real
real unreal.
Do not come too close to me!
I am dance I am song.
Do not make me real!
Reality kills.
The spirit of the dance cannot be captured in a number.
The immaterial cannot become material.
The finely-drawn cannot be made crude.
That which is without artifice cannot be made artificial.
The swift cannot be transformed into the sluggish.
Do not treat me as real!
A paradox cannot be resolved into simpler factors.
A paradox is a paradox
an explanation challenge exhortation
a flame
clear in itself
declaration of love
with no other answer than love
is a synthesis.
In the synthesis the spirit of mobility is
captured
the spirit of the dance.
The synthesis lifts its wings
is mobile in a different way from heavy analysis
it rises above its captured mobility
and is mobile in the mobile in mobility mobile
in every nerve intermediary nerve inner nerve outer nerve
in every nerve-fine nerve's nervous nerve's
nerve of nerve-fineness nerve-resilience
nerve of nervous nervosity that is nerve
that lives nervily nervously nerve-finely
strong-nervedly resilient-nervedly nerve-susceptibly
nerve-sensitively in nerve's nerve-receptivity
in every nerve's nerve that again is nerve
that lives nervily nervously intensely nervily

most nervily in stillest movement
in the unseen play of muscles compelled
muscularly muscular sinewily energetically resiliently
controlledly muscularly museanly musically
sounding silence's movements of stillness.
That is dance. Now I dance it.

I the spirit of winged dance
rise fall fall rise
fly in Indian dance.

Freud

You who do not want to believe
you have never looked into your brains
I have looked into my brain
I have looked into a shaft
I have burrowed in a mine.
Forty years I burrowed
Moses in the desert in a mine
half a human lifetime
until I got there
A trauma lifted
a pressure vanished
I was inside the vein
brilliant gold flowed out.
Half a human lifetime
in order to get there.
I am in the subconscious.
Another half
in order to will the pure.
My patience is long
as the prophet's in the desert.
A cry comes from mountain peaks:
'I am a stranger
in a land that is not my own.'
I am making it my own.
I will only be content
    with the best
the best in man.
Sediment is not water.
I will only be content with water
clear fresh from the primordial source.

'Death analyses'

Death analyses so inexorably in syntheses that vary the varying
theme varied monotonously monotone the varying in the infinite's
nuances develops grows the theme that which was fettered in order
to fetter all over again more and more fetter more clearly more
inexorably fetter the already fettered until caught in the captivity of
the final synthesis it lifts its wings and flies through the transparent
thinness out into the great nothing. Nothingness is all.

Simone Weil

Israelites
people of the exception:
in the depths of the people except
let go under
I do not belong to you.
Human beings human beings only
everywhere human beings not exceptions:
I the daughter of men
am going to the very bottom
lower than God's chosen people
through torment shame
annealed in the fire of the camps gassed gassed to death
I love the human being
in the mine in the shaft
black sweaty sooty
laughing childishly
with hungering thought
playing eyes living.
Do not turn arithmetic into figures
arithmetic is not figures
the arithmetic sings in Greece
sounds in Hellas
do not turn geometry into figures
a vibrating field it shines
listen in through hearing's shell
no longer incomprehensible you will get
silence out:
swift fire of the pulse-beats how it oscillates
pendulates
quiet incalculably not perceptibly not in second
                              far from minute

unassuming.

In vineyards I tread grapes
meet there in the past in Hellas
the human being sun-drenched happy called the Messiah
invisible lonely

to be nameless is to be lonely
to be lonely is to be without form.
Raise raise up!
the position of the people of the exception
there are no exceptions
I deny
I am burning
burning to death
all are equal
suffering makes equal
I give you of my brain
make use make use of that knowledge!
Man cannot be cured
logic does not count in figures
cannot be exterminated you will exterminate man's soul!
Man cannot be turned into a number
arithmetic is something different from numbers.
geometry is something different from shapes.
Only listen:
lives in the logic of the universe
in the love of the universe
must lead to love
to the effacement of the exception.
Raise raise up!
All proud ones are chosen ones
in love humbled transforming logical

Palms of Hands

Palms of hands spread out with no skin
soft kneecaps' command
will not let go of crooked legs
soles of feet yearn for skin
toothless mouth
endless weeping
from wells of sorrow
newborn child.

I Write

I write it shows in the eyes of the dog
it creeps in the paw of the cat
it shimmers in the solitary fly's pair of wings
it leaps in foaling withers
it flies in the flight of birds
it flies
it sinks
in the earth down under roots
it smiles in the infant's eyes
it grows in the eyes of children
it wonders in young eyes
it yearns in human eyes.

FROM **POEMS III**
(1954)

Fragment

— —
— —

In flakes flower-petals change colour
fall off
gums recede
roots throats
shiver uncovered
scurvy ordered forth by the voices of the blood
in the muteness
death-pills fall into fear   life-pills will not go down
death spills   life spills and who is denouncing
who the one   who the other
Radek   Trotsky   Stalin
leader against leader
Führer   il Duce
can anyone give a name to power in human soul
to bring about the destinies
that will turn back into blood and lungs
spiders' webs and shivering
insects' poison
that will weave together
there beyond the doubt of tired eyeballs
a strange knowledge
in league with death-sentences
and curls of hair
like spriggy kindling
to be thrown forward at veils
before face that wants to be covered
and see no more
and lips suffer and burn away
bleed and dry to leather
witches' pyres are lit in the body's interior
burn away all flesh
diluted the blood sings gnats' song
to the rest to be sucked out
in shiverings and headaches
as when an early flower releases its corolla
but still tightly closed in bud

and there come late winter snow and hail
and make the corolla fall
and yet in its roots' secrecy the plant does not give up
it pushes up more flowers
but then comes June with iron nights
gales and intense cold
after a long and rainless spring
and sick and blighted seeds are inhaled in great quantities
even though not visible to human eyes
in an interior enveloped in flower-petals
they fall fall fall
then came a spirit just as heavy
to traverse world and senses
pressing into the smallest crevice of the nursery
messages courtesy of Curie antennae
to the bed where young girl lies outstretched sick
the voice comes violently wakening
anxiety attack   severed contact
with blood that was flowing fresh within veins
and the little sister in the bathroom's mists
stops nail-curved scissors
listens bent to her toes
on the bathroom mat
raises herself on bended knees
presses together the palms of her hands in wordless prayer
with lifted face
eyes caught by play of vapours
yearns towards east and sunrise
while the accusation thunder-like
roars along walls
Reichstag fire
and muteness Indian in passivity
is transferred put to death
serving goals
whose weight and signficance only the person of the action knows
forgotten by the German people
Dürer's method of drawing
with animals and plants the right of hands to work gently
in the service of patience   emulative contours
branches of trees   fine-limbed stems of flowers
rhizomes in topsoil layer
an aged face in chisellings diagonals and corners

wave-lines cross-lines furrows deep folds as on fields
near the ridge of the nose   under eyes   in the forehead's
        threshing-mill
a soil for death's reaper to harvest
bald pate covered by skull-cap
clues everywhere hidden in the beard to unscrew the bottle
out of which the water of life has vanished through a loophole
empty of meaning   laid bare in the autumn of old age
and dead blue-tit
fixed on parchment with rainbow colours
insides of wings   turquoise   Prussian Blue   dark brown
a hint of lilac too
and feet in orange and brown
beak so red with the outside blue
and head light brown
neck hungrily upward-stretched
one might think
the tit is still snapping for air after death
and horseman Death on meek horse
all this was Dürer's method of drawing
but not destroying
the child above all
blue-eyed adorned with flaxen fringe
or dark-eyed brown-haired black
it is all the same
high forehead shy smile and gaze turned away
in the recesses of the library
well-informed from birth
and the ball the terrestrial globe between hands
one supporting it from below
the other placed over it as if to protect
parallel spheres that will never meet
provided that the ball the globe does not
plummet
hurtle   fall
as happened
but the child followed the ball's fate
was carried on women's backs   in gypsy bundles   mass migrations
was gassed beaten to death   kicked
hurled into sewers
thrown from burning houses
by desperate homeless mothers

German Polish Jewish Russian
now without distinction
doomed for racial impurity
never found any refuge
other than cloacas' nether world
there mothers were glad
if sometimes a washroom was opened for them
dirty as in the bistros of southern seaports
with a lavatory hole in the floor
and a device with a grating
for the washing of the inner sexual parts
here they could relieve their bowels or bear the child
which an unknown father of unknown nationality had given them
while they slept unconscious of anything
but dreams of home and gentle stars
and tranquillity's narrow sickle-moon on deep blue late autumn
        nights...
the red of tranquillity no more of war
– the golden sickle-moon of peace –
that rises with the seal of calm and safety
shining over moonlike faces and closed eyes
cut-off hands
hands that belonged to arms resembling flower-stems
and whose palms had vibrated with the delight of working
in their grip between index finger and thumb
with support of middle finger
to clutch a pen or a pencil
to scratch signs and figures
abstract patterns
and hands
that found their joy
in touching
their husband's forehead eyes   lightly over his hair
bringers of joy joy joy
and more joy
had hands like these
hungered thirsted on the insides
wanted to adjust the child's lock of hair
to embrace his foot   protecting the eager one
who always wanted to throw off boot and sock
to take hold of his hands so that the game could go on
to raise him high above her head on upright arms

so that the little one could look down
feel himself on top
and yet safe
at the sight of his mother's face
– and press to herself his defenceless body
breathing in soft complexion of dew
fighting for the health
the unfathomable untouched wisdom in the gaze of his eyes
wanted to hug close to herself
protecting against war contagion and fire
but always there were more wars
where the Jew rose up from the ghettoes and concentration camps
the Israeli was threatened instead
perceived as a threat
by Bedouins without tents homeless ragged
– violence or non-violence   war or non-war
could the world's fate perhaps some day be decided
by women like the Jewish Polish ones all long ago dead
dead with their children
which they held up appealing
before the terrible one
Aryan in power and glory
divested of all power's insignia
but power in its pure state
power for power's sake
naked power
he stood
among them
dismounting from his horse
finally smiling
considering almost tenderly
those eyes woken by horror   turned away
not daring to look at the bare-stabbing face
only supplicating: 'give us – let us keep our children'
and he   quiet   seemingly affectionate
depicted   everywhere visible on walls
surrounded by smiling hordes of children
here with a resolution in his back pocket:
'I will send your children to bath-houses and gas ovens
and make you into slaves' –
but these women are dead
their children suffocated

amd those women who now live with knowledge
live with another knowledge
another experience
that of pettiness
that of competition
are themselves suffocating their own and others' children
spiritually
for the sake of an extravagant dress
for one more mine
or one more yours
if one child can sing
an injustice has been done to the other that was not born with a
        singing voice
so must each generation
undergo anew
the same heavy experience
mingled blood shame and tears
where woman betrays
maternal feeling
her own or her sisters'
the spirit that was triumphant in Poland
is doubly triumphant in posterity

_ _
_ _
_ _

[1954]

FROM **IN HEAVY CLUSTERS THE BERRIES RIPEN**

(1959)

Retrospect

Insomnia meets insomnia
and is confronted by a new thing
desolation meets desolation
and grinds an empty mill
silence meets silence
but they do not recognise each other
the discord is double
dull and broken the silences

I am chilled to the soul
to the consistency of my body
sometimes in the consistency
shattered lines appear
– and I remember a burial ground in North Africa
consisting of broken columns
melancholy beautiful presences –
dented is that which has no contour
dented the unknown
whose only certainty is
to be something undefined
in itself without contour
with the need to remain something undefined undefinable
definition imparts a purpose
and a dent
while truth flees
a limitation
knowledge's this far but no further
barbed wire and fencing or atom bomb
imprisonment or annihilation
truth they do not deliver
policemen or doctors
policemen and doctors
since they have proved to be the same thing
I am chilled to the soul
since the laws of heredity
have been thus outwardly confirmed
I am in pain

When I returned to my home town
I was met only by inherited experiences
empty space and fencing
distress and electric charge in the unknown
it is obvious that human beings
follow a law of repetition
that has nothing to do
with heredity as such
I no longer believe in anything
here I find it desolate
brutally inhuman
'every night Black Majas' stop
outside your door'
the children in the courtyard shout
to the child
embarrassing for committees embarrassing for parents
embarrassing for police embarrassing for ambulances
not embarrassing
with the deep transparency of crystal
in itself
that which scarcely exists
or exists among the embarrassing ones caught in outside the world's
embarrassing breaks and intersecting lines
'every night'
shout the children
and I feel myself deeply attached
to the one who is being addressed
his eyes reconnoitre
by day with the sleepless gaze of the watcher
his hands shake like a polio victim's
though he is trying to recover
and learn the ways
the ones that do not separate
the guffaws the derision the invective
the tricks
'us lot' the proof of those fit for existence
that they are within their rights

they have made it up and are plucking
withered flowers out of the rubbish bins
and I see before me a funeral procession
as I saw it more than twenty years ago

when I was reading Bellman
I see again the lemon-yellow tints
in the black and the white
and perceive again
the eternal recurrence
with fresh recognition as though it were for the first time
I realise
that it is that yellow colour
that constitutes the streak of the macabre
forms tone and foundation in this whole
even though it is the black and the white
that dominate
while the yellow exists as dwindling
distant flecks
but

'Moses, you that killed our Jesus'
scream further back in time
the flax-fringed boys to the Jewish boy
in front of the staircase in the inward-turned crescent
a primordial cavern
that the sun found
and the most prickly cactus
they beat him
and his eyes accept more and more the suffering
slightly contemptuous and very reticent expression
I thought was Christ's

look now they have beaten his face to blood
and at the same time and suddenly a large rat brushes
against my feet
where I stand pressed against the wall
with a trembling of revulsion
caused by the rat

someone comes out onto the staircase crosses the street
stops and ties his bootlaces by the wooden fence
the Jewish boy has gone
but from the many who remain come
more clever remarks calls shouts
Jews live on the block
but antisemitism seethes in this street

– which are the Jews? –
and rats tumble out
from the small holes in the wall
– not only the Jews
even though there is this punctuality
and morality –
from the basements
– the homes of the Jews
are particularly clean
they have shown me it:
shining linen
and holders with candles
before the bread and the flour and the drink
and they must not eat that which is fat –
there are ghosts in the dark passages
far below the holes
that lead to them
though one does not want to believe it
now outside
there people creep on all fours
old women with grey locks of hair
amidst rats and damp
no doubt there are also preserves there
in tidy cupboards behind lock and key
and clean piles of firewood
behind more carelessly guarded doors with lattice-work
and chinks
and fallen pieces of wood in the passages
people hit each other over the head with them
at night
when there are fights
that make the house shake –

go down there in the daytime
come across turns and labyrinths
running transverse to the wall
and in shrieking mute spirals
that which at night rose
from the lowest and noisiest
through the many floors
then muffled more audibly again
until the two heavy iron doors of the two right at the top

that hold back
clean laundry hanging up to dry
and stores of naphthalene large chests
old books
crippled furniture
small windows that give an inkling of sky
openings towards air and light
here the spirals meet hope and silence
and flee
but the abandoned secret passages let one breathe
one could live in them
as long as the spirals
did not sink again

but if they sink through everything
and through asphalt
and through stones
somewhere there will be earth and black soil
hidden gardens and murmuring boughs
cities and new houses
fresh water colours and gaudy bits of paper
scraps that pieced together form a world
transparent as those long clusters
glass pearls
or grapes
hard to know which
they are there also scattered out and gathered in heaps
perhaps this is all there would be:
grapes and glass pearls
gaudy scraps of paper
and one large piece of paper
scissors and adhesive
so it may be put together
a substance different from glue
in the adhesive a clarity as in light

that lonely red pearl
has received a scratch
a crack that makes visible a paler tint
from fissures caverns well
pearls and more pearls
that have not appeared
in fragments and whole

as in the lake below the wooden fence
fragments and pieces of glass
now that it is spring and the bottom reveals
what the winter has preserved and washed clean:
a red tin can and a colourless formless thing here and there
among the debris
rusty nails

nine hours Christ suffered on the cross
then he asked for water
and they soaked a sponge in vinegar
and said: drink!
that is the worst part
of the story
I consider
and am seven or eight years old
I grow younger and older
like Alice in the book

cold tea
when one is sick and has a fever
drinks dreams

all the while the same street is in question
but I listen and look away from everything
even from the pond's bottom now
towards other streets or towards the end of the street
where there are grass hills and at last
a bay facing the sea
in the other direction in towards the town up the hill
there is only a rock
it shimmers inaccessible sparkles beautiful far inside
a basement vault's rocky dilapidation
like a lamp it assuages perhaps
the spirals of fear in that house
and lights the nightlight
of comfort and alleviation
there are other roads
but one takes that road often
on account of the rock

without any time of day
free from the disturbing tick of clockwork

and death-heavy hollow tollings
the one who sits on the top deck of a bus in London may
get up
and jump down feet first
and land on her feet
without anything else happening
other than the police making a note
that the possible cause
of a traffic obstruction
has taken place

a child jumps from mountain ledge
to mountain ledge
if no one has warned it
if no one has made it aware
but warned made aware
it hesitates experiences long in advance
or first
the forced inactivity of the muscles
the nerves' vigilance
                              and often falls
instead of jumping

in the warning is concealed
the suggestion

in the denial
half the affirmation

and the one who acts
contrary to the warning
follows the suggestion
experiences half
the confirmation
in the denial
experiences the words
and the words in the words

an oblivion so deep
a knowledge so wide
a sleep so lacking presence
and dream

inaccessible
like theirs who died long ago
and are presence
with them
for them
for theirs was wordless gain
slow and difficult
their insights

now Hölderlin's pear shimmers
and has penetrated
Chinese wisdom
the frontier of the arbitrary
and returned
with Dürer's Italian pear
and that blemished rotating pear
of worthless metal
freshly rolled from its hiding place
a plaything
enticing to the four-year-old child
and that absent-minded recognition
until it recognises and hears
tenaciously
the long warning that dwells inside the object:
'not yours – not yours!'
and the rolling back to hiding-place and captivity

autumn wind hunts across the earth
and half of life
is cold
is loss
the yellow spot on the eyeball
and spots of emptiness
from the gaze
to the bare walls
with the gaze
over the desolate walls

half of life
– unutterably tortured poet –
was utterable
but was held back

was too separate
and also too valid
only not with words' common usage
fragments and truth
and in the fragments truth
hiatuses and tentative honesty
soaring flight weight
now missiles hiss above Korea
– my child goes to kindergarten
and every minute is indignant
but in every bead shimmers a world
and in the next waiting one
shines a world –
three-, four-year-olds at kindergarten
are sullen resigned hopeful
expectant disappointed sad indignant
almost without break and even in moments of boredom
indignant
sometimes tired to death
if a dog gives a bark
or a car a shrill sound of its horn
they may easily be run over

I wrote a poem about Korea
it was not whole
I tear it up
and piece together each constituent part
tear it up
and write become no one
my poem shall no longer be a poem
it shall be 'the tearing-up of a poem'[2]

for children going to kindergarten is
a stabbingly violent acquaintance with emotional anonymity
during so and so many hours
with becoming-anonymous becoming-no one
and the next day again
day after day for the greater part of the day: to be no one
a drop in the ocean
to be born to exist a short while and be effaced
to work gloomily: to play
consume a prescribed portion

neither more nor less
and on their return home be less and less someone
more and more the others

and yet stubbornly perceive that something stubbornly persists
and is the same thing
its existence presupposes that a someone too exists

one sees it in a mirror
one smiles at it one speaks to it
one makes an effort in order to be able to like it
one studies its garments
pretty altered that have been someone else's
one speaks to this one and that
one smiles at this one and that
one wishes it new ones
completely its own which no one has yet had
and the wish comes true
Then one suddenly becomes one with the image
is assailed by emotion
that's me isn't it
and flees

For the one who is homeless the right thing
to do now would be
to write one word in one corner of the paper at the top
the other right at the bottom of the sheet in the opposite corner
and in between let
the abyss yawn

one eye fell down into the well
another flew up to heaven [3]

Korea and yet not Korea
not Korea and yet Korea
doctoral dissertations
yellow parchment against white and black

there were those
who worked at abolishing
the preconditions of cruelty
from Bellman to Westermarck

a notebook
from more than twenty years ago[4]
from Schiller and Nietzsche
from Almqvist and Södergran
and fear and trembling
at this present moment Korea's
and seven years later
– – –

life consists of present continuous
moments
their tense remains present

the violently approaching future
has a hostile effect
and is thrown off
in so far as is possible
its tense
remains a desired perfect

the unknown that approaches
with recognition influences
deepens one's own

it was not foreseen
by those who sought to perceive
the justification and non-justification of prejudices
the roots and rootlessnesses of religions
a cruelty like this
every bit as though it were a matter of
plucking healthy teeth out of the soul
the knowledge with the superstition
the knowledge of everyday experience along
    with the ignorance
the vitally essential memories with the painful ones
my fatherland is my fatherland
I think
(with the accents of a ten-year-old)
and add
shall so remain

and in Korea

experiences that are different divide
those that are the same bring understanding
awaken humour reason tolerance

Korea – similar people
it is with similar reactions
the circumstances that strictly speaking are not perhaps so different

what is humour? the resigned face of the animal
the resigned faces of certain poems
the gentle movements of the deer
swift fleeting and sympathetic
connections
inside fences be they ever so wide apart
the open fixed gaze of the mother deer
and the slumbering reflective gaze of the deer calf
then unanimous
craning of necks
much is unutterable
even in poems
which no one speaks aloud any longer
more than halfway
who will reach forth pearls
be they ever so genuine
and assiduously
revised
by pain
once received

only the one who still hopes
and the one who is chivalrous

the resigned face of the child
conscious milk teeth

avoir une dent de lait contre[5]
to have a milk tooth against someone something
to have one's milk teeth against
to have aching milk teeth even though not against
to have them neither for nor against
only conscious
sometimes aching

a compound
a multiplicity
the characteristics of situations
of preconditions
a saint could not misunderstand

the unique the solitary that exists in everything in everyone
the Jewish boy's smiling
way of tying
way of selling shoelaces on a street a harbour edge
a pavement pressed against a wall
way of making paper butterflies in solitude
green pink blue
for completely selfish ends
for the simple sake of staying alive

selling them in a café – a pavement-edge
in a gateway pressed against a wall
– those were always the friendly ones –

ability to endure
(ability to accuse without it being plain
whom the accusation concerns
the doctor the doctors?
but they are nearly always the last
to be concerned or involved
most often and nearest to hand are
the pre- and pro-doctors instead of the doctors
they are the ones who get there first
with their: 'admit that such and such is the case
the deterioration the relapse'
in order afterwards to say: 'well, what did I tell you'
          and nowadays fire-hoses even machine-guns
in place of enemas
tanks in place of thoughts
and ability to accuse so it is always plain
whom the accusation concerns
the unique the solitary
the undefined the undefinable
the in existence itself in itself existing
the in and for itself undeserved
intransigent not expressible

innocent
its guilt is poverty
or will to a self-responsible
a stubborn clinging
to life
non-expressible
and flight escape with possible refuge
in the quest the wandering
towards something undefinable
perhaps really God
not death
but freedom
yet sometimes death
when death is more merciful than life
when death has room for that which human beings no longer
have even a loophole open for
something supra-personal something non-human
something non-figurative and non-imaginable
and not accessible to the senses

avoir la forme enfoncée dans la matière[6]
the spirit in the matter
the form in the content
the soul in the wine
the wine in the form
the spirit clear as the wine
is not the drunkard said to be with God
God grant protection to the drunkard
and is not the child's consciousness naturally intoxicated
does not each child incessantly prove
the presence of a supra-personal superhuman protection
the existence of a continuing miracle
even though it may hurt:

a dinghy
in a storm
threatening to capsize
the remains of disappearance
white in darkening grey
or that of a butterfly carefree
to fly whither it will
even though space is charged

with the influences
of the approaching lightning
of the imminent deluge

struck by non-figurative death
but not by a wingless antennae-less life
it sinks it falls that
which the lightning splits
the violent rain crumbles to dust

the spirit in the soul in the summing up
in the almost without substance or body
but has it not also been a question of
unwittingly provoking revulsion
by not allowing the keeping of blind motives
the senseless motives of cruelty

a childish directness may have the effect
of a ruthlessly honest naturalness
it constantly overturns human morality
divisions into motives to be affirmed and denied

Watteau's *L'Indifferent* in shimmering yellow
Bellman's funeral cortège
Mozart's C and D
Villon's 'The Ballad of the Hanged'
which without the least waste of time
with the cool delight of the spring
serves up truth
self-evident birdsong
even though pecked and eaten by birds
with the rope dangling around his neck
jester in green and yellow
the unique the solitary
which a few seconds centuries earlier
was the spring's oblation
sometimes ready for mutual death
a few seconds centuries later
the child's dismayed smile
when it died of wounds this morning in Korea
its sudden indifference
as its face turned pale

yellow against the black hair
so indifferent was the encounter
with the knowledge of the powerful
in a land where the many cultures have met together
in order to liberate enrich teach cure
penetrate   with violence   cause   illness   and   splitting

but then also cure
civilise help
but with knowledge for death
lemon-yellow skin against black wisps
'they say what does not need to be said
they make visible what does not need to be made visible'
eyes so turned-away that only the whites are prepared to meet

experience of mutilation of the irreconcilable
and yet capacity for reconciliation
if not with those who were experienced irreconcilable
then with one's own and irreconcilable
laughter's inner lines
in the sudden emphases indifference
the smile or merely the grimace
that leaves out the bitterness
in the flower death flowers too
equally valid
the natural certainty
the familiarity
deeper than knowledge
than incessant knowledge can allow
dizzying excruciating insights
concerning validity
that is allied with death
and will endure beyond it
they too are grounds for consolation
everywhere the guilt is unprovable
but everywhere it is also provable
how the child sees [7]

the tone's retaining quality
in the colours
even there scarcely existent
objects are dead

yet the sight of the inkpot on the table
the absent-minded contemplation
which possibly does not even know it is contemplating
can recall
the memory of similar inkpots
decades ago
but living or at least inexpressibility –
radiating intermediary inkpots
and not facts
but states of mind
everyday objects
that must frequently be renewed
contacts with forms and colours
and beyond the forms and the colours
the way characters are written and print
there are cold
and catching cold
a bridge and a heap of stones
tattered stockings and a snowdrift
the quenching of thirst and white snow
that falls into children's palms
and slowly becomes soft slush
that they shape
and make love to with the tips of their tongues
all the way to their gullets
until they feel the thirst rising
the ink that in the summers
dried in the abandoned inkpot
while one wished it was fresh and longed
for the time when the snow fell
and for the darkness
lit by the glow of log fires
their quiet music
and the warmth that flowed towards one
when the protecting doors were opened
it was Christmas
and embroideries
but why always with prescribed patterns
one would wonder afterwards
connected with the embroideries
there was
the world of pale colours

of pastels
and chalks
in unopened boxes of school supplies
they sometimes sent out forewarnings
unanswered
but just as allied to embroideries as to pale colours
Fredrika Bremer's world
sewing girls through rows of books
alongside the *Thousand and One Nights*
books that smelt differently from other books
with colours that were different
and non-pictures
the scent of fresh-baked rolls
Kantianly rational
shaped like rolls
not like animals or human beings

writing round the ink-bottles in two languages
an ambiguity that acts inwardly
if one of the languages is left out
the unambiguity seems half and cruel
yields loss without depth
symptoms with violence force hatred
reservoirs prejudices
and judgements
often in the evenings one must pray
to the 'God that loveth'
of homelessness and longing
and into that awkward 'loveth'
mix meekness's decent breakfast porridge
the neither too thin with half-cooked groats
nor too thick
speak Chinese or Korean
but not Finnish
write in French but not in Swedish
speak impure Spanish Moorish French but not French
and not Swedish and not Finnish
above all not Swedish and not Finnish
European
an anthology of European
non-Europeanness
to be at odds with one's time

means
to abandon all languages
to speak argot dialect slang
languages too have their border regions
which only the child crosses with sure insight
or the philologist within strict margins
but for those who have been wholly thrown back on
the fragile threads of words
'danger for wearying dancers' feet,
danger for weakening climbers' arms' (Södergran: 'Scherzo')
how many in the fairytale
on their way towards the talking bird up there on the mountain
the singing tree the golden lake
turned the screaming the mockery the derision
into black statues
only the girl who renounced
accessibility to hear
got there, she who renounced speech
and with trust offered pearls like nourishment
letting pearls and birds apportion truth

Are there not poems
from primordial souls Van Goghian flames
conceptions
knowledge sights visions colours
it is what has scarcely yet been born
or has been born and reborn through many thousands of years of
transformations
that which however oppressed
silenced
by the weight of threshing-machines or tractors
mown down trampled down
yet always rises up again
in order once more almost to be
almost be seen
almost be heard

this music runs parallel
seems from relative connections
relative points of view to melt together
but does not touch barely brushes
and melts together nowhere

from the perspective of the finite
it seems
reconcilable
with that of the infinite
but is not reconcilable
is not reconciled
it is a line an arc a hyperbola
that sails out dizzyingly alone
brushing dilapidated graves
Almqvist's major minor major
Bach
towards completion
and yet not
were minor only to express sorrow
major only joy
how narrow music would be
how distorted and trivial
relatively expressible
the connection
one could cry
out into the mauve unpleasantly streaked night
the nauseatingly green
migraine-charged half:

this pillow is too thin
here and there only rough cloth
this bed-quilt is too repulsively
ugly
cold and hard
a sketch of curses
the unkindness that falls to the lot
of the poor and the homeless
a covering of distress and fear
a surly pledge
that falls over and moves to the edge
a persistent reminder that
it is from poverty
endless poison spews out endless
corroding venom

but yet it is not shouted
perhaps only because indifference's

alpha
always happens
when the shout has died away
should it turn into its opposite
say: all the same
apathetically
the reminder involves
if not exactly kindness
then at least
the attempt at it
and something better than nothing
is after all of interest
and what negations
could not the too tender
in case it were in question
evoke
in this night
in essence always again
the thousand and one
and the same anew new
with sudden alleviations
oases and springs
(only dreams and halfway between waking and dream
guileless untiring bring new things)
one can see
the most indifferent
shadows
Bellman's 'passengers'
swaying
but whether
from drunkenness tiredness or illness
know only those
who too quickly always know
acting after the event
judging apathetically
according to effects
but not preconditions

it used to be called
oppressors and oppressed
will it now be called:
carers and cared-for

144

how much more detestable
the hypocrisy the pharisaism the lies
the torture no longer a thousand and one
but undemonstrably endless
have had their chance
to multiply and choke
the truth that could only have endured
with responsibility to a superhuman being

indifferent yet not apathetic
God or freedom
in this night that can rise towards heaven
sink underground
give the music admittance
the colours the symbols
the visions
the reminder of freedom
is the only reminder of value
freedom is worth its price
as long as it exists
first it then the preconditions

the dressmaker's sleepless ones
in a bus
here in Paris in Marrakesh or in London
it is she who is in question

it is day
and the precondition of the one who writes
is to have slept
so it is not I
it is no matter whom
the anonymous one
the anonymous ones

their faces are grey
with all that divides

freedom is to roam
as one's thoughts move
as they prescribe oblivion
and select from among the visible

it is to sit in a bus
to look without looking
at the careworn face
the hollowed-out faces in the same bus
the person's
not the factory worker's not the office worker's not the fashion
        shop assistant's
or precisely theirs but also something more in each
something indifferent that does not fit in
does not match any given or accepted descriptions
does not match the situation
and yet already inseparably
belongs together with this
fleeting and fleeing
escaping
of actual situations
the original situation exists
only barely or scarcely at all
and there exists
something indifferent
irreconcilable with any kind of existence

each dawn new
able to be warded off with a newspaper pre-cooked food
the strenuous use of a piece of hope a scrap of resignation
out of life's grey sludge
it is this that is life
it is the miracle
the continuing lasting miracle
the endurance is the miracle
the triumph
that brings sudden alleviations
and also the triumph over the revulsion
the one that is inherent in life

to scratch a cypher
write a logarithm
draw five broken lines
trace a circle or a square
pray to God
as individual cost and effort

triumph
preparation before
a world collapses

and is forgotten
because of dirt that takes over the skin's pores
because of grease that takes over
the hands of the woman who washes dishes
because of the needle-stab
that takes over the inner world of the embroideress's forehead
and the inner world of her eyes
because of the hopeless search of the unemployed
because of the completed disgrace of the invalid
in a world where only grace

only the unemployed and the invalid
know life
experience wholly

in pain the dirt can be felt
in pain are the grease the dust the fumes of refuse
matter's and then also
the nausea that proceeds
from the more immaterial
the snubs the jokes the talk the words
the grimaces and the grimaces in the tone of voice
in the pain are the dirt are the stains
the definable and analysable ones

each day to travel through increasing pain
which towards evening ebbs away
this is what life is
even if one does not immediately recognise it
and it is the sleepless night
with dewy freshnesses
and dreams midway between sleep and wakefulness
midway between reality and vision
even though not immediately recognised so far down
in the roots of childhood in fresh black earth
through the grey river
whose muddy bottom-substance
greets one with numbness towards death

whose
the revulsion at the utterances
of the subconscious
when with frivolous explanations
the compassion of the moment
merciless and cold
to the welfare of others
it stabs souls
that were born too whole

the victim's revulsion at violence
what can surpass it:
not the child's revulsion
not that of the helpless
and not that of knowing better the revulsion of real knowledge
before the actions of ignorance
not the revulsion of the prophet
before deliberate obduracy
provocation of evil

no nothing can surpass the revulsion
caused by the unrepentant violence of the strong
against the weaker
only Cassandra's clear-eyed
trembling
that took unto itself
and included
the child's the seer's the prisoner's
the condemned man's
the slave's and the rape victim's
trembling
can have surpassed
and preceded it

are there not also those
who share the life of the worms
the life of the mice
the life of the moles
the worm considered as worm
the mouse as mouse
the mole as mole
without invested human meanings

they have no power
either as individuals or as a group
they are perhaps 'not of this world'
together the others form the power
as individuals their power is nothing
at most the word could be fleetingly valued
and even then provided with a minus sign –
but together or a few together
they are power
if they address these who scarcely exist
it happens via the police
but only freedom exists
freedom or God
who sees through everything

the one who loves God
praises in hospital:
the bare walls
the empty outside wall surfaces
the inhospitable interiors
and the unfriendly faces even
the sour treatment
they nourish the instinct to remain
free
they drive one towards the exit
make it possible to find the keys that used correctly
will open the doors
for those who are called mentally ill
by those who above all and everywhere
believe themselves to be mentally well

but if the impossibility is of a physical nature
and it is plain
that it often is
it is a question of a hospital like any other
merely of people who are ill
except that no one knows what kind of illness it is
nor knows the cure
but do not call it incurable
do not say: lock them up
for the rest of their lives
and drive out all the

pre-doctors pro-doctors
instead of the doctors
so that the patient is at least allowed to know
who the doctor is
these people know nothing and think they know everything
their assumptions and hypotheses
are false
of them all that can be saved is their own humanity
their authority is based on what might occur to them
if the situation was theirs
but not even that can be known with any certainty
experience is half of the knowable

there is only a disaster
helplessness
and a soul that bleeds
fettered

an ever-growing disaster
far outside
beyond reach
but conditional
dependent

'in order to avoid the atoms' struggle'
'all my atoms are separate
and on fire' [8]
every atom in me is in revolt
every atom in me is ceaselessly influenced

what in man
is the work of the atoms
how do they function?
and when existence stops
man dies
what happens?
how does the work of the atoms continue
in man
how do they keep on –

what concern me are poems
written under the influence of atoms

the others concern me not at all
nowadays
atomised poems have existed
for as long as the world has existed
and paintings music
of atoms' influence

built of globes
this circus-girl[9]
with the wise good sense
to give up understanding
in order then to raise a lever
with iron poles
on upstretched arms
and the effect of sovereign
resolve without cramp
not
even in thought
ever once to diverge
from the rondel

or without fear
with knowledge from frontier
meeting wide-open gaze
girl in diagonal[9]
and those honest
leaves in the background
impure stains on poems
exist
because of immediate reality
do not write: it ought in itself
but: in itself
but hidden by what
and obscured

when every atom is affected
by reminders and hostility
helplessness and unavoidability
the receptivity of the senses increases
existence is desired
without smell without taste without colour
take everything away

so that I can see[10]
be silent
so that I can hear
movement ceases
and even the most imperceptible one
all vaporise

it is they after all that proclaim
to life
from the planet Mars
to the sun that actualises them
extinguish all life –
or extinguish me –
into the absolute blackness of the musical scale
that takes
draws to itself
all sun –

if the run-through is over
I shall wake up pierced through
if life is again
woken to new consciousness
everything will be dew-fresh
and with colours smells forms

it is a question of matter
if existence
that must go on in spite of destiny
because of destiny
is not determination
unknown in the same degree as given
for each and all
the attempts to diverge
the runnings-away
were worth the apologies

something too small
against something too great
almost not substance matter
portals open on every sickness
every shortage
on every surplus too

on every atom in change influenceable
inflowing energy

the meaning
the one that is given to man:
the composition of the atoms
in a world
that experiences the composition of the atoms
without perceptible will to acknowledge
a higher conscience
justification
without respect for life
and without respect for death
without acknowledgement of one elementary
universally valid principle
for human beings without distinction
in what is elementary and universally valid

if only the world were to change
many things
and I too would change
if only a will to knowledge without destruction
existed
if only Blake's visions of more subtle human beings
a lever with iron poles
would lift out of people
the weight

the individual is a particle
in an endless connection
solitary and dependent on everything
a lie for the sake of the end
alters the connection
but remains a lie
affects everyday weekday
the normal

a murder for the sake of the end
affects the chains of causes
affects with accents of violence
what happens in the street on the road
in normality everywhere

violence for the sake of the end
even though concealed
remains violence
and gives rise to more violence
violence is a crime against freedom
those who love their own freedom
do not commit violence
do not mock

God does not resort to violence
in knowledge
that paradise
with all that belongs to it
preceded by violence
would be the inferno

I am chilled to the connection
to the composition
until I remember
that one must say to oneself and repeat:
love your freedom
love it then God too will become comprehensible
then no irreparable evil can befall you
the one who says freedom instead of God
can be brought low only by death

love freedom
because of that and only because of that
the hardest and the easiest

dark red grow the berries
in heavy clusters
on bearing boughs
allotted more summer more energy
in darkness and light
sweetness grows
they ripen
worlds
black without end through gleaming
depth and blackness

NOTES:

1. 'Black Maja' is the Finnish name for a 'Black Maria'.
2. Södergran: 'Resolve'.
3. From my: *Theme with Variations.*
4. An old notebook: dating from 1934, it is mostly concerned with Nietzsche's *Ecce Homo*, Södergran, Schiller's *On Realism and Idealism*, Bellman, Almqvist's *The Literature of the Old and the New*, *Some Brushstrokes: The Natural in Art* and *On Man's Support*, Kierkegaard's *Fear and Trembling* and some more about Bellman and Södergran.
5. Molière: dent de lait 'c'est que vous avez, mon frère, une dent de lait contre lui' (Argan to Béralde in *Le malade imaginaire*).
6. La forme enfoncée dans la matière (Cathos in Molière's *Les précieuses ridicules*, refers to an idea of Aristoteles, whom Molière allows his character to misinterpret).
7. Björling formulates the problem like this in a poem: 'how children see' ('Our Cat-Life Hours').
8. Södergran: 'Materialism' and 'Ecstasy'.
9. Painting by Schjerfbeck: 'The Circus Girl' and in the passage that follows 'The Girl from Eydtkuhnen'.
10. Valéry: Otez toute chose que j'y voie. Valéry's ideas about the most extreme shade of black in 'Log-Book de M. Teste' find a parallel in Schjerfbeck's reflections on colour. My lines mostly describe experiences of extra-sensory states and working with colour

Complete Poems
KARIN BOYE
TRANSLATED BY DAVID McDUFF

Karin Boye is Sweden's greatest woman poet. Born in 1900, she was far ahead of her time, and her controversial writings included the novel *Crisis*, in which she depicted the religious turmoil of her adolescence and her discovery of her own bisexuality. In her early poems, she is a tense modern spirit aroused to strenuous affirmations of absolute ethical loyalties. Her identification with nature's dark but knowing and fertile instincts is more complete in her later work, in which serene nature symbolism is mixed with ominously strained elements.

She rose above personal defeats to write with clarity of vision and nobility of utterance. Her poetry has a strenuously angular quality which reflects – with naked candour – the harsh realities of her tragic inner struggle, which was to lead to her suicide in 1941.

Complete Poems
EDITH SÖDERGRAN
TRANSLATED BY DAVID McDUFF

When she died in poverty at 31, Edith Södergran (1892-1923) had been dismissed as a mad, megalomaniac aristocrat by most of her Finnish contemporaries. Today she is regarded as Finland's greatest modern poet. Her poems – written in Swedish – are intensely visionary, and have been compared with Rimbaud's, yet they also show deep affinities with Russian poetry. The driving force of her poetry was her struggle against TB. For much of her short life she was a semi-invalid in sanatoria in Finland and Switzerland.

Edith Södergran saw herself as an inspired free spirit of a new order, a disciple on her own terms of Nietzsche, then of the nature mystic Rudolf Steiner, and finally of Christ. But her voice is subtle and wholly original. It transcends the limits imposed by her illness to make lyrical statements about the violence and darkness of the modern world – imagistic poems that are alarming in the surreal beauty of their fragmentary diction.

Ice Around Our Lips
FINLAND-SWEDISH POETRY
TRANSLATED BY DAVID McDUFF

Much of the literature of Finland is written in Swedish, for Finland was a province of Sweden until the 19th century. This illustrated anthology has selections by ten major Finland-Swedish poets, from the *fin de siècle* figure of Bertel Gripenberg to "separatist" poet Gösta Ågren. Between them come the austere Arvid Mörne, avant-gardists like Edith Södergran, Elmer Diktonius and Rabbe Enckell, the much celebrated living poets Bo Carpelan, Solveig von Schoultz and Claes Andersson, and Gunnar Björling, Scandinavia's only dadaist.

Isolation is a central theme in Finland-Swedish poetry. Yet while these writers may be obsessed by loneliness and melancholy, their work is full of vitality, surprisingly different and sharply aware of the rest of European literature.

Contemporary Finnish Poetry
TRANSLATED BY HERBERT LOMAS
Poetry Book Society Translation Award

This anthology traces the history of post-war Finnish poetry, with a comprehensive introduction, and selections by 21 poets from Eeva-Liisa Manner (born 1921) to Satu Salminiitty (born 1959), and with the most space and commentary given to the two major Finnish poets, Paavo Haavikko and Pentti Saarikoski. Among the book's surprises are the animal parables of Kirsi Kunnas, Finland's Stevie Smith, and the satires of Jarkko Laine, whose work is fuelled by a hatred of conventional poetry and religion.

'This is the most brilliant and exciting anthology I've ever read. As brilliant in its poetic standard and range as in its translations and editorship...The tone is tough and sophisticated, the style tremendously spare and witty. Many English poets would do well to study it...These translations rise to a height hitherto unreached. Fiercely colloquial, magical as any shaman's words, visionary as legend, Lomas's art offers us a magnificent feast from Finland, in yet another handsome volume from Bloodaxe' – ANNE BORN, *Ambit*

A Valley in the Midst of Violence
GÖSTA ÅGREN
TRANSLATED BY DAVID McDUFF
Poetry Book Society Recommended Translation
& TLS Bernard Shaw Prize

Ågren has developed an intellectually austere form of aphorism-lyric, which in its concentration and imagistic density looks both inwards to the metaphysical traditions of Finland-Swedish modernism and outwards to contemporary English-language poetry, especially that of R.S. Thomas. His work is featured in David McDuff's Finland-Swedish anthology *Ice Around Our Lips*:

'Gösta Ågren is the real discovery: an Ostrobothnian quasi-separatist Marxist, he is heavily influenced by R.S. Thomas, but his taut, muscley, short lines remind me, too, of Edward Bond, prismed through a totally Finland-Swedish consciousness...Gösta Ågren has absorbed his modernist predecessors...tough, but compassionate... abstract and imagistic and sensual. He feels like a major poet' – ADAM THORPE, *Poetry Review*

Wings of Hope and Daring
EIRA STENBERG
TRANSLATED BY HERBERT LOMAS

The Finnish poet Eira Stenberg writes mainly about home life, about sexual and family politics, but she deals with family relationships like an exorcist casting out demons. She views the conflicts of marriage, divorce, motherhood and childhood with a ruthless eye.

The male may meet a hostile, disenchanted eye, a levelled carving knife, but the mother too must see its point, and the rather demonic child. There are also more overt gestures to the larger family: 'The concentration camps are set up at home.' In spite of her tragic view, her poetry can be tender and playful. Hers is a deadly mind, but the deadliness springs from a lively love of life. Her work is a tool for locating the enemies of happiness, whether these are decomposing ideas, family history, psychological cesspools or institutions. 'Whatever the antonym of sentimentality is, she has it' – HERBERT LOMAS

Collected Poems
TOMAS TRANSTRÖMER
TRANSLATED BY ROBIN FULTON

Tomas Tranströmer is Sweden's most important living poet. Also a professional psychologist, he has been called a 'buzzard poet' in Sweden because he sees the world from a height, in a mystic dimension, but brings every detail of the natural world into sharp focus. His poems are often explorations of the borderland between sleep and waking, between the conscious and dreaming states. 'A single-minded, obstinate search back to a pristine sensibility that actually belongs in childhood' – JOANNA BANKIER.

'A poet of exceptional achievement has with this volume been born into English' – MARTIN DODSWORTH, *Guardian*. 'This is a *Collected* to read, re-read and absorb, and Robin Fulton's translations render these memorable poems with accuracy and empathy' – ALAN BROWNJOHN, *Poetry Review*. 'A book to keep under one's pillow so that, like Charlemagine and his notebooks, it might teach one how to write. And see' – ADAM THORPE, *The Literary Review*

Snow Leopard
TUA FORSSTRÖM
TRANSLATED BY DAVID McDUFF
Poetry Book Society Recommended Translation

Tua Forsström's poems are remarkable for their directness and emotional courage, her deeply musical voice seeming to speak out of the fabric of existence itself, its utterance organised and structured through a compactness and density of diction.

'Forsström's lines have the icy intensity of the great Edith Söd-ergran and the aphoristic as well as the mystical qualities of the Finland-Swedish tradition, but McDuff's translations indicate a fragility that is wholly particular. While Forsström's visions of loneliness and despair are tempered by a lyrical pluckiness, the abiding mood is of dissolution only just kept in check. They have the tenderness of snow, of Penelope's "bones like porcelain", or of "the loved ones who walk with us in the smoke/ of our breath".' – ADAM THORPE, *Observer*